'Do you really go, Beth?'

She looked at his mouth while he spoke, finding it difficult to register the words he was saying. He was close, close enough for her to feel his warm breath on her face, and it was all she could do not to melt completely into his arms. Her tongue came out to wet her lips as she flicked her gaze up to his eyes, knowing the desire she saw there mirrored her own.

She swallowed. 'No.'

He gazed down into her eyes and slowly nodded. 'I didn't think so.'

C000121026

Lucy Clark began writing romance in her early teens and immediately knew she'd found her 'calling' in life. After working as a secretary in a busy teaching hospital, she turned her hand to writing medical romance. She currently lives in South Australia with her husband and two children. Lucy largely credits her writing success to the support of her husband, family and friends.

Recent titles by the same author:

CHRISTMAS-DAY FIANCÉE
COMING HOME TO KATOOMBA
  Blue Mountains A&E
CRISIS AT KATOOMBA HOSPITAL
  Blue Mountains A&E

A KNIGHT TO
HOLD ON TO

BY
LUCY CLARK

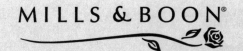

MILLS & BOON®

To Cassie & Lisa, for picking me up
when I'm down and feeding me chocolate!
1 John 4:10

DID YOU PURCHASE THIS BOOK WITHOUT A COVER?

If you did, you should be aware it is **stolen property** as it was reported *unsold and destroyed* by a retailer. Neither the author nor the publisher has received any payment for this book.

All the characters in this book have no existence outside the imagination of the author, and have no relation whatsoever to anyone bearing the same name or names. They are not even distantly inspired by any individual known or unknown to the author, and all the incidents are pure invention.

All Rights Reserved including the right of reproduction in whole or in part in any form. This edition is published by arrangement with Harlequin Enterprises II B.V. The text of this publication or any part thereof may not be reproduced or transmitted in any form or by any means, electronic or mechanical, including photocopying, recording, storage in an information retrieval system, or otherwise, without the written permission of the publisher.

This book is sold subject to the condition that it shall not, by way of trade or otherwise, be lent, resold, hired out or otherwise circulated without the prior consent of the publisher in any form of binding or cover other than that in which it is published and without a similar condition including this condition being imposed on the subsequent purchaser.

MILLS & BOON and MILLS & BOON with the Rose Device are registered trademarks of the publisher.

First published in Great Britain 2006
Harlequin Mills & Boon Limited,
Eton House, 18-24 Paradise Road, Richmond, Surrey TW9 1SR

© Lucy Clark 2006

ISBN 0 263 84724 1

Set in Times Roman 10 on 11¼ pt.
03-0406-57058

Printed and bound in Spain
by Litografia Rosés, S.A., Barcelona

CHAPTER ONE

'How are you feeling?' Tristan asked as he brought over a cup of coffee. 'Here, drink this.'

'No. I can't. It'll just churn in my stomach and make me feel worse.' Beth held up a hand, warding off the coffee-cup.

'How much have you slept all week?' He sat down beside her. Thankfully the doctors' tearoom in the emergency theatre block was empty except for the two of them. They'd just come out after five hours of surgery and it was almost eight o'clock in the morning.

'Hardly anything.'

'From one friend to another, sweetheart, it's starting to show.'

'I'll sleep tonight. It'll be over by tonight.'

'It's not that bad, surely.'

'Tristan, the man I thought I'd never see again is starting work at the hospital in...' She glanced at the clock on the wall '...seven minutes' time.'

'Officially,' Tristan clarified.

'I don't feel well. You're a doctor. Can I go home sick? Quick. Write me a sick certificate.'

Tristan laughed and shoved her head between her knees. 'Stay there for a few minutes, then take two paracetamol and don't call me in the morning.'

Beth lifted her head. 'Oh, you're a riot. Here I am in the middle of my biggest crisis and you're making jokes.'

'Why is Sir Ryan Cooper working here such a big deal to you?'

'I've told you. We shared a…a…moment at the Christmas dinner last year.'

'That was over six months ago, Beth. He's been working in London, you've been working in America. You've just returned and he's come home to Sydney. He's working here, he's your boss and he seems like a decent enough guy. What's the big?'

Beth raised her eyebrows and chuckled. 'What's the big?' she repeated, amazed. 'Learned that from your daughter?'

He smiled. 'What can I say? She's twelve.'

'Well, hip daddy, the "big"…' She made the inverted commas sign with her fingers '…as you call it, is that it's not good to insult the man who might one day be your boss.'

'Or "share a moment" with him.' Tristan made the same hand gesture. 'Just relax. I'm sure Natalie would tell you the same thing if she wasn't so caught up in wedding preparations. How's that going, by the way?'

'Almost there. Five more days and then she's Mrs Marty Williams…or is that Dr Marty Williams? Dr Natalie Williams?' She looked at her friend, a puzzled look on her face.

Tristan patted her head and stood. 'Too much for your tired little brain to compute right now. We'd better go. Ward round time. Don't want to make a bad impression on the new boss.'

Beth groaned again, feeling her stomach churn once more.

'Hey, look on the bright side.'

'There is one?'

'Thanks to Sir Ryan, Richard Everley's in London for the next twelve months.'

Beth laughed. 'I can always count on you to find a silver lining.'

'Hey, you're talking to a man who shares a house with his wife and four daughters. Silver linings are my speciality.'

There was no reason to change out of their theatre scrubs as once ward round was done, they were both due back in Theatre for the elective list. 'Do you think Sir Ryan will join us in Theatre?' Beth asked as they walked towards the ward.

'He might. Think you can handle the pressure?'

'Will you hold my hand?'

'Might not be the most effective way to operate. Just think, in six more months we'll both be qualified orthopaedic surgeons.'

'If I live that long.' She groaned and shook her head. As they entered the ward, she went through some mental exercises to calm her nerves. At the nurses' station, she closed her eyes and took a few deep breaths. She'd just managed to get herself under control when she sensed someone was watching her. Slowly, she opened her eyes and looked right into the blue gaze of Sir Ryan Cooper.

'Long night in Theatre, Dr Durant?'

She opened her mouth to speak but nothing came out. She closed it again, cleared her throat and forced a smile. 'Not really.'

'Glad to hear it.'

They both stood staring at each other and it was as though the past six months had melted away and they were back in the restaurant at Christmastime. The chemistry between them was still there, alive and more potent than before. How was that possible? She'd only seen this man a few times and she knew next to nothing about him.

Ryan forced himself to breathe and as he did, he was treated to the most tantalising perfume…Beth's perfume. The woman was enough to drive him completely to distraction. Her hair was longer than it had been at Christmas and was pulled back from her face in a no-nonsense ponytail. Her eyes had dark rings around them, testifying to a late night, or rather, he corrected himself, an early morning. Still, even though she was dressed in theatre scrubs, she looked incredibly sexy, as though she'd just got out of bed. He liked what he saw more than he cared to admit.

He broke the gaze, working hard at controlling his thoughts. This…whatever it was between them couldn't go anywhere. She was his colleague and he knew of old that work-based relationships never worked. He was starting off in a new hospital, with an excruciating workload, and there would be absolutely no time for a social life, despite the irrepressible tug he felt to gather her into his arms and plant his lips firmly over her own.

Now that he'd broken the gaze, Beth found she could focus a little more clearly. The moment was over. They'd seen each other, she'd realised the attraction was as strong as ever and there was nothing either of them were going to do about it. He was an arrogant and overbearing surgeon and she was a registrar attached to his unit. That's all.

'Welcome back, Sir Ryan.' Tristan walked into the nurses' station and held out his hand to Ryan, giving Beth time to slip away. She could have kissed Tristan for rescuing her. She headed over to the ward conference room where they started ward rounds, discussing interesting cases and necessary treatments before they set off to see the patients.

She smiled at her colleagues and sat down, realising belatedly that her hands were shaking. She clenched them together, holding them tight. Ryan and Tristan walked in together. Tristan said something and Ryan smiled, not a smile that met his eyes but, still, the way it relaxed his features just for that moment was enough to make her breath catch in her throat. Did the man have to be so…so…good-looking? So…irresistible?

Ryan called for quiet and then introduced himself, getting the ward round under way. Beth forced herself to focus. Today's round would take longer than usual because Ryan would be given a complete update on every patient in the ward by the treating doctor. He asked questions and gave comments, showing his obvious experience in their speciality.

When it was her turn, Beth shoved all thoughts of the attraction she felt for Ryan out of the way and concentrated on what she was saying.

'Do you think that's the correct treatment for Mrs Harding?' Ryan questioned.

Beth glared at him for a moment. Was he trying to put her down? To discredit her in front of her colleagues? She swallowed and looked down at the case notes, quickly scanning the treatment she'd prescribed. Raising her head, she met his gaze and held it. 'Yes, I do.'

'Good. I agree.'

Was that a test? Had he just tested her? Her blood began to boil but once more she kept it under control. When they finally came to Mrs Harding's bed, Beth watched in astonishment as Sir Ryan smiled and charmed the elderly woman, and she was pleased to note he had a wonderful bedside manner. Some of the more brilliant and accomplished doctors weren't very good with patient contact, even though they were experts in the operating theatre. It was nice to see this side of Sir Ryan, even though the way he smiled at Mrs Harding only made him look more handsome. Beth growled, knowing this would make the man harder to resist. Almost an hour later, when the round had finally finished, she fled the ward, heading up to elective Theatres, needing to put distance between herself and her new boss.

'Whoa. Hold up there,' Tristan said, finally catching up with her. 'What's wrong?'

'Nothing.'

'Beth. I know you better than that.'

'Then you'll know what's wrong without asking.' She wasn't going to mention her reaction to Sir Ryan's smiles and tried to recall the earlier anger she'd felt.

'He wasn't picking on you.'

'No. He was testing me.'

'So? That's his job, Beth. He's the big boss and he needs to know what levels his staff are on. Besides, you're one to talk about tests.'

'Meaning?'

'Have you forgotten your little check-list?'

'That's completely different.'

'No, it's not.' They walked into the doctors' tearoom and Beth grabbed a cup and made some coffee.

'It is, so. We're talking about life-altering decisions here, not second-guessing doctors.'

'I'd say second-guessing doctors could well fall into the life-altering category,' Tristan mumbled.

'No. *My* check-list is so I can find the man of my dreams. Someone who understands not only me but my parents as well.'

'I don't see what the problem is. Your parents are dwarfs. So what? They're fantastic people.'

Beth felt her anger slip away and she smiled at Tristan. 'Why aren't there more men like you out there?'

'There are,' he said softly, placing his hand on her shoulder. 'You'll find the right guy. Just don't go tarring and feathering the new chief right away. He might surprise you.' Tristan turned away and helped himself to a biscuit.

'He's as arrogant as they come and I can't stand arrogance.'

'You think he's arrogant?

'Absolutely.'

Tristan merely shrugged. 'Perhaps there's a reason behind that.'

'What do you mean?'

Tristan put his arm around Beth's shoulders. 'Nothing. Just don't judge him too quickly.'

Beth looked down at her coffee-cup, her annoyance with Ryan melting away. Tristan was right…as usual. She smiled up at him. 'Thanks.'

'Preparing for your operating list?' Ryan's deep voice washed over them and Beth snapped her head around to look at him standing in the doorway, dressed in theatre scrubs. How long had he been there? Had he heard them talking about him? Ryan glared at the two of them, specifically at Tristan's arm about her shoulders.

'Are you joining us?' Tristan asked.

'Yes.'

Tristan smiled and removed his arm. 'Coffee before we begin?'

'I'll get it.' Ryan didn't look at Tristan, his eyes still boring into Beth's. 'In fact, I have a job for you, Tristan.' He finally transferred his gaze to the other registrar. 'If you go see my secretary, Jocelyn, she'll give you the details.'

'So I can play my "get out of Theatre free" card?'

Ryan nodded.

Tristan's grin increased as he glanced at Beth. 'Looks as though your test isn't over.' He turned back to Ryan. 'When do I get tested?'

'I'll operate with you tomorrow, if that suits?'

'Sure thing, boss.' Tristan, turned and winked at Beth. 'I'll catch you later.' In the next moment he'd gone, closing the door behind him, which left just Ryan and herself…and the incredible sense of electricity crackling in the air between them.

They were alone in the room and where Beth usually wished for privacy when she was in here, she now wished it would fill up with people.

Ryan seemed to realise that standing there, staring at her, wasn't going to do him much good so he walked over to the bench and opened a cupboard. 'Can I take any mug?'

'So long as you wash it afterwards.' Beth shifted away, trying to put some distance between them.

'Tristan seems like a nice person.'

'He is.'

'His personnel file says he's married.'

'That's right. He has four girls. Lots of oestrogen in his household.'

Ryan looked over his shoulder. 'You know his wife?'

'Juliette? Of course. Tris and I have been working together for the past two years.'

'Except for the last six months which you spent in California, I believe.'

'Yes.' Beth eyed him coolly. 'Is anything wrong?'

'No. No. So you're just friends, then?'

Beth bristled. 'You think I'd have an affair with a married man?'

'I don't know. I hardly know you, Beth.'

'Well, for your information, I wouldn't.'

He took a sip of his coffee and nodded. 'Good to know.'

'You know, contrary to popular belief, men and women can be friends. Besides, I don't date people I work with.'

'Really?' His eyebrows hit his hairline. 'That's not what I've heard.'

Beth was stung. 'Listening to gossip on your first day?'

'Hardly.'

'Meaning?'

'I accidentally overheard.'

'Overheard what?'

'Two men talking about you in the change rooms.'

'Should I be flattered?'

'They seemed quite impressed you were back.'

'So?'

'Well, I don't want to alarm you with the details but a bet was made.'

Beth's hands began to tremble again and she quickly slumped down into the chair, placing her cup on the floor beside her. She buried her face in her hands for a moment before lifting her head to look at him. She was surprised to find him crouching down just near her, not having heard him move.

'What did they say?'

'That they'd have you out on a date within the next fortnight. Whoever gets the first date wins.'

Beth closed her eyes and shook her head.

'This doesn't seem to be such a surprise to you.' His voice was gentle and she realised the man she'd shared those few moments with at Christmas had finally resurfaced.

She dragged in a deep breath and opened her eyes. 'I used to do what I call standard-dating. Before my trip to America, that is. I guess you could say it's my personalised form of speed-dating.'

'Why?'

She shrugged. 'Why does anyone speed-date? They've been hurt before.'

'Not necessarily.' He pulled a chair over and sat down. 'It's not like those organised events where you have five minutes to "make a connection"?'

'No. Although I have done that, too.'

'So you just go out on dates?'

'Yes. If things don't work out after that first date, then I don't go out on another. I'm not into wasting time, hence the term "standard" dating.'

'And you can tell from one date?'

'I'm very picky.'

'So if a man passes the first date, he gets a second?'

'Perhaps.'

Ryan was looking at her with a strange look in his eyes, as though the idea appealed to him way too much and he was willing to give it a shot. 'You didn't get in on the bet, did you?' she asked warily.

He smiled…a broad smile that touched his eyes and made them sparkle. 'No. Should I?'

Beth swallowed, feeling her mouth go dry with anticipation. Was Ryan making a pass at her? Her heart started pounding wildly against her ribs and her lips parted to allow the pent-up air to escape.

Why did she have this reaction each time he turned on the charm like this? It wasn't fair! She didn't want to be attracted to Ryan Cooper but it appeared she was and it was much easier to fight that attraction when he was being arrogant, overbearing and dictatorial.

The smile had slowly disappeared from his face and he was now looking at her rather expectantly, obviously waiting for her to answer the question he'd asked. Now, if only she could remember what it was.

The door to the room opened and the anaesthetist stuck his head around. Beth shifted back into her chair, feeling guilty for some strange reason. 'There you are, Beth.'

'Hey, Joey.'

'Your first patient's arrived. I'm just on my way to see him.'

'Thanks. Er, Joey, have you met Sir Ryan Cooper?'

'Sure. We just met in the changing rooms.'

Beth's eyes widened. 'Is that so?' Joey was one of the men who wanted to date her? She was surprised because he really wasn't her type at all. 'OK. I'll be there soon.'

Joey nodded and headed out, closing the door behind him.

'Interested in Joey?' Ryan asked, standing up and taking her coffee-cup to the sink. He threw away the undrunk contents of their drinks and washed the cups.

'I told you, I don't date colleagues.'

'Any more.'

'Any more,' she agreed.

He nodded but looked at her as though he didn't believe a word she said. 'We'd better get to Theatre.'

'Good idea.' Beth stood, hoping her legs would support her as she headed to the door. Thankfully they did. Ryan was right behind her.

'There's just one thing I want to know.'

She turned and looked at him expectantly.

'Why don't you date colleagues?' he asked

'Too risky.'

Ryan held the door for her, looking down as she passed him. She made the mistake of pausing, belatedly realising just how close they were. She gazed up into his eyes and dragged in a breath, his fresh scent winding its way around her and making her knees go weak.

'Dr Durant, I completely concur.' His tone was soft, intimate, and she liked it. 'Now, get moving to Theatres before my resolve breaks and I ignore both our rules about getting involved with a colleague.'

Beth's jaw dropped open in shock. Had Sir Ryan Cooper just admitted what she thought he'd admitted? She couldn't move. Her gaze searched his, wondering whether she'd merely thought he'd said what he'd said.

'Beth,' he warned, and this time she found the strength to move, hurtling through the doorway, directly into the path of another colleague. She apologised profusely as she headed up the corridor, feeling heat emanating from Ryan's body behind her.

'Don't say things like that,' she said briskly.

'It's the truth.' His voice was very soft but his words were clear enough for only her to hear. 'I've wanted to kiss you since the Christmas party but you're right. Now is definitely not the time, or the place.' She stopped dead still at his words and his shoulder collided with hers. He placed his hand beneath her elbow and forced her to keep moving. 'After work? Today? Are you free?'

Beth glanced at him, not sure whether to take him seriously. 'You sure you're not in on this bet?'

'Hardly.' He wasn't going to admit the thought of those other men taking her out had driven him wild with anger and envy. Then he'd walked into the tearoom and found Tristan with his arm about her. Ryan shook his head, knowing he had to focus.

They reached their patient and stopped walking. 'We'll discuss it later,' he said briskly, and Beth watched as he switched personas. Gone was Ryan, the cute guy she could grow to like…and in his place was Sir Ryan Cooper, her arrogant, overbearing and definitely annoying boss.

'Great,' she mumbled. 'Why couldn't I get the cute one in Theatre?' She headed over to her patient. 'Mr Sommerfield. How are you feeling?' She looked down at him.

'Woozy.'

She smiled. 'Good. Looks as though the pre-med is doing its job. I'm going to get ready and I'll see you in Theatre.' Leaving her patient to the nursing staff and anaesthetist, Beth headed to the scrub sink where Ryan was already methodically scrubbing his hands. She didn't say a word, even though she was highly conscious of him, of every move he was making. There was one thing she knew she had to do and that was to pull herself together before the operation began. Not only was he going to be assisting her, he was also going to be testing her.

'I've arranged for two interns attached to the orthopaedic unit to come into Theatre and watch. They haven't seen a total hip replacement done before,' Ryan said by way of small talk.

'I hope they have strong constitutions,' she retorted, not at all pleased at the audience. Normally it didn't bother her but she could have done without the extra pressure.

'If they want to become surgeons, they'll have to develop one,' was all he said, and that was as far as the conversation went. Once they were scrubbed, she almost had her mind under control. When they put on balaclavas and face protectors, she was totally in the 'surgical zone'. The fact that she could hardly see Ryan's face helped a lot.

As she walked into Theatre, Ryan, the interns, everything faded into the background as she focused on the job she had to do. They prepared the patient, making sure he was in the correct position, that he was stabilized, and Beth began the sterilising and draping procedures.

She explained what she was doing to the interns, knowing this was the main reason Ryan had asked them here—to test her on her verbal training skills. 'Now we're ready for the incision. As you can see, the hip is flexed to twenty degrees and adducted across the contralateral thigh. I'll make a straight incision centred over the greater trochanter, three finger breadths above and five below the level of the trochanter.' This she did. 'Next, the fascia is incised at the same level as the trochanter and then split proximally and distally, with the gluteus maximus split in the line of the fibres. The secret is to split all bursal tissue over the trochanteric region.'

The interns, who were standing to the side of the theatre in a non-sterile area, were watching intently, scribbling notes on bits of paper. Beth continued with the operation, describing aloud every step she was performing. Ryan asked a question here and there but for the most part he assisted her perfectly, pre-empting her needs as she would have expected from a surgeon of his calibre.

When it was time to carefully dislocate the hip by adduction and internal rotation across the other thigh, Ryan was there to assist and hold the patient's leg at a ninety-degree angle to stabilise it.

'Thank you,' she murmured.

'You're more than welcome,' he replied, his voice equally soft. Her gaze flicked up to meet his but although his voice had the smooth, delicious tones of Ryan, the penetrating gaze was that of Sir Ryan and it was enough to bring her mind back into focus.

Later, once the operation had been completed, Beth sat in the female change rooms and buried her head in her hands. How could she have lost focus in the middle of an operation? She'd let Ryan's voice unnerve her and she simply wasn't used to things like that happening. If his eyes had been soft and filled with desire, she may have lost her focus completely.

'You're a professional,' she told herself sternly as she stood and looked at her reflection in the mirror. 'You hardly know the man and, whether or not there is anything between you, there's no reason in the world why you should let it interfere with your patients.'

'Talking to yourself, Beth?'

Beth looked over to where Lisa, one of the radiologists, stood watching her.

'And who is the man who has you in such a tizz?' Lisa's eyes lit with merriment.

Beth groaned and shook her head. 'He not only has me talking to myself, he's got me talking to my reflection.' She smiled and looked at her friend. 'Which theatre are you working in?'

'Two, and you still haven't answered my question.'

'I doubt it would take you long to guess.'

'The new ortho boss?'

Beth smiled but didn't confirm or deny it.

'Isn't he Marty's cousin?' Lisa continued.

'Yes.'

'Is he as good-looking as Marty?'

'Yeah. I guess he is.' She sighed.

'You guess?' Lisa raised her eyebrows. 'He must be one humdinger of a looker if he's got you talking to yourself in the mirror.'

Beth smiled again. 'I'd better get back to it. I still have three patients to do and I have two interns observing, not to mention Sir Ryan's eyes glaring into me, watching every move and probably hoping I make a mistake.'

'Sounds like fun times for you.'

'And then some. I'll see you at the wedding if not before.'

'Oh, yeah, how's Natalie going? All wedding preparations under control?'

'Basically. We're all staying in a posh hotel this week—Natalie, her mum and me.'

'Oh, that's right. She had to give up the lease on your townhouse. Where are you going to live?'

'Well, Natalie said I could house sit while she and Marty are on their honeymoon, which gives me three weeks to find some-where to rent.' She headed towards the door.

'If I hear of anywhere, I'll let you know.'

'Thanks, I'd appreciate it. Now, if you'll excuse me, I have to go have loads more fun, fun, fun.'

'You doctors really know how to party,' Lisa called with a laugh as Beth headed back to theatre three, which was hers for the rest of the morning.

'Dr Durant.' She turned and found herself face to face with one of the interns. He was over six feet tall and was looking at her with admiration and a touch of hero-worship. 'I'd just like to say thanks for explaining everything so clearly during that to-tal hip replacement.'

'You're welcome.' She smiled politely at him.

'I've never been in an orthopaedic theatre before but that was really great.'

'What rotation have you just finished?'

'Neurosurgical.'

'How did you find it?' She pointed towards her theatre. 'Sorry. Do you mind walking with me? I need to get this list moving.'

'Uh…sure. Uh…well, I liked neurosurgery but after that op-eration, I'm very interested in orthopaedics.'

Her smile was genuine this time. 'It's rewarding, so long as you don't mind the grinding and bone-crunching parts. Are you staying around for the rest of the list?'

He sadly shook his head. 'I'm scheduled to be down in A and E but I'll be in clinic this afternoon.'

'OK. I'll see you then.'

'Great…er, and thanks again.'

'My pleasure.' She headed over to theatre sister and had a few words with her before checking on her next patient. She hadn't seen any sign of Ryan since the last operation had finished and she wondered whether he was going to go and torture someone else. By the time she stood at the scrub sink, there was still no sign of him. She breathed out a sigh, not sure whether it was from disappointment or relief.

'He's a little young for you,' a voice said from behind her, but she didn't need to look over her shoulder to figure out who was there.

'I didn't think you were going to continue to grace me with your presence.'

'Don't change the subject.'

'What subject was that, Sir Ryan?'

'The intern. I saw you talking to him.'

'Heaven forbid,' she joked.

'He's a little young for you,' he reiterated.

'Only by about four or so years. That's not much.' She lifted her eyes to meet his, raising her eyebrows as though encouraging him to retort. Thankfully, he didn't. He merely frowned and flicked on a tap.

'What's left on the list?'

'Arthroscopic synovectomy, bilateral arthroscopic release and an arthroscopy.'

'Good. Shouldn't take too long.'

'If you have somewhere you'd rather be…' She trailed off and when he gave her a bored look she shrugged her shoulders. 'Can't blame a girl for trying.'

'Do you want to get rid of me?'

Beth breathed in deeply and considered him for a moment. This was a much easier way to deal with him, she realised. Just treat everything as a joke and his arrogance seemed to wash right over her. 'That all depends on whether or not you're going to behave yourself.'

It was Ryan's turn to raise his eyebrows. 'This is how you speak to your new boss?'

'Looks that way to me. What are you going to do? Kick me off the rotation?'

'I might.'

She smiled at him. 'Should I be scared?'

'Of me?' Ryan found it difficult to swallow. This was the first time he'd seen her in this teasing, light-hearted mood and he liked it…*a lot*. 'Or of being kicked off?'

'You pick.' She elbowed off the taps and picked up a sterile drape before sauntering off to get gowned and gloved.

Ryan continued to scrub, knowing full well there was a silly grin on his face but for the first time in a long time he couldn't wipe it off. It was ridiculous that a woman, especially one he hardly knew, could draw him out of his shell like this. At work he preferred keeping his distance from his staff, he found it helped, but those few minutes exchanging friendly banter with Beth had made him feel as he had before Geraldine had ripped his heart out, before he'd seen the horrors of war and before his knighthood.

Yes, he felt good.

CHAPTER TWO

THEATRE proved to be uneventful, with Ryan definitely behaving himself. As the interns weren't around any more, she no longer had to explain every step she made so she and Ryan worked in a companionable manner, the strains of Chopin playing in the background.

'One of your favourite composers?' Ryan asked as they degowned after the last operation.

'Classical music's relaxing in Theatre.'

'But not your first choice if you were going out dancing?'

'Who says I dance?' She collected the notes and sat down to write up her report.

'Well, with your dating record, you would have certainly taken to the floor more than once.'

Beth shrugged and concentrated on what she had to write. When she'd finished she closed the notes and looked up at him still standing there. 'I like rock, jazz, most types of music really.'

'You like jazz?'

'Sure. Why?'

'I don't know. Usually it's an acquired taste. People either like or loathe it.'

'And what about you? Like or loathe?'

'Neither. Love is more the word I'd use to describe my feelings towards it.'

She raised her eyebrows at the look on his face. It was one of pure pleasure, of peace and relaxation. 'It sounds as though you're more *involved* with it than just loving it.'

He smiled down at her and this time she was terribly glad to be sitting. The effects, the full effects of Ryan Cooper's smile, his twinkling blue eyes and the way his entire body seemed to radiate happiness filled Beth with a sense of…*wow*.

This man would be lethal when he really turned on the charm and she'd better start preparing her heart to fight it because she already knew she liked it when his attention was focused on her in this way.

'I guess you could say that.'

His gaze meshed with hers and this time there was a real connection between them. The other times they'd been locked in this manner, it had been more of an awareness, but not this time. This time, it was more…more because Ryan had actually shared something personal with her.

Beth's beeper sounded and she checked the number and groaned, tossing down the pen she was still holding. 'Clinic. And here I thought I was going to get a lunch-break today.' When she looked back at Ryan, it was as though someone had shut out the sunlight. His face was composed once more.

'Snowed under in clinic, are they? Right. I'll go get changed.' With that, he headed out, leaving Beth to frown at his retreating back. She only sat there for a few minutes before she was disturbed by the nursing staff who wanted to get everything sorted out and ready for the next operation.

Beth rang through to clinic and spoke to Tristan. 'So, how'd it go?' her friend asked.

'OK, I guess.'

'You sound real enthused.'

'What's there to be excited about?' she bantered.

'Come to clinic and find out.'

'Really? It's that exciting there?'

'More than you can believe. Is Sir Ryan coming?'

'He's already on his way. I'm going to change and then I'll join in the fun.'

'See you then,' Tristan replied, before Beth hung up. She sighed as she headed downstairs to the emergency theatres changing rooms, where she'd left her clothes earlier that morning. After a quick shower, she dressed in her black trousers and pink top. She was just passing through A and E when one of the triage sisters grabbed her.

'We've got a case about to arrive that I'd like you to review, Beth. Do you have time?'

'Sure. Do you mind calling Tristan in clinic and telling him I'll be a little later than planned?'

'OK.'

'So, what's the case?'

'Ice-hockey player.'

'In the middle of the day?'

'Professional athlete.'

'Not being seen by his own sports doctor?'

'We're the closest hospital and apparently he's pretty bad. You'll have to put up with the team doctor and any other heavies he brings with him.'

'No problem. Been there, done that.'

Sister paused for a moment. 'Think they'll ask for the head of unit?'

Beth closed her eyes and sighed, realising that was a valid point. She looked at her colleague. 'Don't worry about calling clinic. I'll do it and get Sir Ryan to come down.'

'All right. Ambulance is due in approximately three minutes and here's the report we've received so far.' Sister handed her a piece of paper before disappearing back to her job. Beth shook her head and went to the nurses' station, reaching for a phone.

'Tris,' she said when he answered. 'I got caught in A and E. Case they need looking at and I'm the happy on-call doctor today.'

'Lucky you.'

'I'm going to need Ryan down here. There'll be big-wigs and all sorts of people throwing their weight around and no doubt demanding to see him.'

'Ryan? You call him Ryan? During business hours? Did he invite you to call him Ryan? What aren't you telling me, Beth? What's really going on with you two?'

'Tristan!' She chuckled. 'Ryan is his name, you dolt. Now, just send him down.'

'You're no fun,' Tristan mumbled. 'All right. I'll send *Sir Ryan* down to you.'

'Thank you.' She hung up and buried her head in her hands. 'Why is this happening?' she mumbled, then felt a hand on her shoulder and turned to look. 'Marty! Hi. What are you doing here? I thought you were on leave.'

'Just finishing up a case that came in. I've sent my newest patient to the paediatric ward and am now going to leave her in the care of my colleagues. I have better things to do, like go and see my bride-to-be.'

Beth smiled. 'Get those flowers organised, don't forget to pick up your tux and, above all, remember to pick out a present for the bridesmaid.'

'Yep. I think that sums up the check-list for today.'

'Only five more sleeps until the big day.'

'That's five more sleeps too many. How's Ryan settling in? I haven't had a chance to catch up with him.'

'He should be on his way down but I'll be whisking him away the moment he gets here.'

Marty raised his eyebrows teasingly. 'Really? Whisking him away, eh? I'm sure he'd like that.'

'Cut it out. We're colleagues.'

'R-i-i-ght.' Marty drawled the word and Beth had the feeling he didn't quite believe her.

She dragged in a breath. 'So, are you sticking around or going to see Natalie?'

'I'm going, I'm going.' He laughed. As he headed out of the department Ryan walked in, the two men passing each other and briefly sharing a hearty back-slap. Beth watched them exchange a few words before both of them looked her way. She instantly cringed and looked down at the piece of paper in front of her, trying to control not only her erratic heartbeat but also the blush she could feel rising.

A moment later Ryan was by her side, his mask back in place. 'What's the situation?'

'Uh…' Beth found it hard to look at him so instead focused on the information. 'Twenty-two-year-old ice-hockey player, male, being brought in with shoulder and neck injuries.'

'Spine?'

'It doesn't say anything about his spine but I'd guess that may have had some damage done to it, too. The team doctor and other…er…ice-hockey dignitaries will be accompanying their star player so Triage Sister and I thought it best if you were here as they'd probably want to speak to the head of unit anyway.' Finally, she raised her gaze to his.

They looked at each other and Beth swallowed nervously, unsure which persona she was going to get. Ryan nodded. 'Good call,' was all he said, before the ambulance siren could be heard. Beth stood and the two of them walked in the direction of their newest patient.

'What have we got?' Ryan asked as the paramedics wheeled the stretcher into trauma room one.

'Andrew Jackovich. Twenty-two-year-old male, collided on the ice and sustained possible fractures to the right shoulder, right arm, right hand, right patella. No loss of consciousness, no signs of internal injuries, although right groin is tender. Blood loss minimal. Oxygen sats ninety-eight percent. No known allergies and patient has taken paracetamol and codeine.'

As the paramedic gave the report, they transferred Andrew from the paramedic stretcher to the barouche bed in the trauma room.

'I'm Dr Smithers,' a man said, walking in from the emergency entrance. 'I'm the team's doctor. I've given Andrew a quick examination but thought it best to leave the poking and prodding to you lot.'

Beth smiled. 'Very considerate of you.' She grabbed a pair of the heavy-duty scissors they kept in A and E and began cutting away the cloth of Andrew's practice uniform. He was well padded up but those pads needed to disappear if she was going to be able to assess him properly.

'Hi, Andrew. I'm Dr Cooper.' Ryan looked down at his patient. 'Care to tell me what happened?' Ryan asked, taking a penlight torch from his pocket and checking Andrew's pupils. 'I think we'll take this off for now.' He removed the oxygen mask.

'I was training,' Andrew mumbled, his teeth clenched together due to the cervical collar. 'Do you have to cut that off?' He indicated his uniform. 'Coach won't be too happy.'

Beth ignored him and kept doing her job.

'I heard it was colliding, as well as training,' Ryan said. 'What did you collide with?'

'The wall.' Andrew grimaced. 'Can we take this collar thing off my neck? It's really annoying.'

'Not yet. We'll just make sure you're all right then get you off to X-Ray. Once we have the all-clear that there's nothing wrong with your spine, we'll think about getting it off your neck. So you collided with the wall. Slide?'

'Yeah. It happens.'

'I remember.'

'You've played hockey?' It was Beth who asked the question as she started checking Andrew's injuries.

'During high school,' Ryan replied.

Beth filed that piece of inconsequential information away and continued with her examination of their patient, calling out her findings so the scribe nurse could write the information up on a whiteboard and get the X-ray request forms organised. The sooner the red tape was tied up, the better. They needed this guy in Radiology sooner rather than later.

'Where is he?' The loud, booming voice came from down the corridor. 'He's my star player. I demand to see him.'

A moment later, a tall man with thinning grey hair and a walrus moustache was shown into the room.

'Coach.' Andrew closed his eyes.

'What have they done to your uniform?' the coach bellowed. Beth raised her eyebrows. It was always nice to see concern shown in the proper proportions. 'The cost of replacing it will be charged to the hospital,' he continued, before glaring at the team's doctor. 'What's the verdict, Smithers?'

'Too early to tell yet, Coach. The good doctors here are taking care of him.'

The coach turned to face Ryan. 'And who are you?'

Ryan didn't stop his assessment of Andrew. 'Sir Ryan Cooper, head of the orthopaedic unit here at St Gregory's.'

As he said his title, Beth was glad she'd asked him to be there when Andrew arrived. If the coach had been bellowing at her, although she wouldn't have liked it one bit, she'd have handled it. Now, though, the bellowing was directed at Ryan but she could see that the coach was impressed with Ryan's title.

'Did you say *Sir?*' Coach's eyes widened. 'Well, that makes all the difference, then.' He turned his attention to his player. 'See, we've got you the best. Fix him up, *Sir* Doc.'

Beth could feel Ryan bristling and she wondered why. The coach continued talking and Beth wished he'd leave so they could get on with their job. As it was, most of the staff ignored him, concentrating on what needed to be done.

'So, Andrew.' Ryan turned his full attention back to his patient. 'You were in a slide and collided with the wall.'

'That's a lot of damage for a collision with the wall,' Beth said.

'An uncontrolled slide can cause quite a lot of damage, as we're seeing here,' Ryan said. 'They can reach speeds up to approximately twenty-four kilometres per hour, Dr Durant. That's quite fast across cold, slick ice.' Ryan hooked the stethoscope into his ears and listened to Andrew's chest. 'All seems clear there. If you're satisfied, Beth, we'll get him off to X-Ray to see what we're dealing with.'

'OK. At the moment, that right shoulder looks as though it may be dislocated. If it is, it's not a bad dislocation but still one we'd need to look into.' She checked Andrew's legs and received the appropriate responses. 'That's a good sign.'

'I know,' Andrew said in a bored tone. 'Don't go thinking this is my first trip to the emergency room, Doc.'

The coach was still bending the ear of one of the staff but now he stopped talking and came over to Andrew. 'Just how many injuries have you had? Was this disclosed in the contract you signed?'

'Yes.' Andrew glared at his coach, then looked almost pleadingly at Ryan.

'Right, Coach. We need you to wait outside. Andrew's not a little boy and we're more than capable of taking care of him without you hovering around.'

'I do not hover,' the coach bellowed. Dr Smithers came across and put a hand on the coach's shoulder.

'Let's get some coffee. Andrew's going to be a while in X-Ray.'

A moment later, there was silence. 'Is he a good coach?' Ryan asked.

'The best. That's why he's such—' He broke off, groaning in pain as Beth palpated the groin area.

'Sorry,' she murmured. 'Feels as though you've pulled a muscle but we'll get an ultrasound of the area just to make sure.' She nodded to the scribe nurse who quickly made a note of it.

'How are his vitals?' Ryan asked Sister.

'Oxygen levels are fine, BP is slightly elevated, respiratory rate is normal, pupils equal and reacting to light.'

'I'm fairly certain you have no spinal injury and there's no sign of concussion, especially as you've retained consciousness the whole time.'

'So I can take this thing off?' Andrew glanced down, indicating the cervical collar.

'I'd still like to look at the X-rays before that happens,' Ryan said. 'Beth? You satisfied?'

'Yes.' She pulled off her gloves and tossed them into a bin before holding out her hand for the forms she needed to sign. 'Let's get you off to X-Ray, Andrew.' Their patient was wheeled away and she took the file to the nurses' station and sat down to finish writing it up.

'Beth.' Ryan's voice directly behind her startled her and she quickly looked up at him.

'Yes?' She jumped a little and placed her hand on her chest. His gaze followed the action before he met her eyes.

Beth was looking at him with a mixture of delight and wariness and he wasn't quite sure how that made him feel. He didn't like the fact that she set him on edge as much as he apparently set her on edge. He breathed deeply, calling on his professionalism to get him through. 'Sorry. Didn't mean to scare you.' Great, Cooper. Real professional, he taunted himself.

Beth sighed, the action causing her lips to part, and Ryan wanted nothing more than to reach out and tenderly touch her lips, with his thumb, with his fingertips, with his mouth. He swallowed, wondering if he'd ever be able to stop gazing at his registrar without fighting the need to kiss her.

She held his gaze for a moment, waiting for her heartbeat to return to normal. She knew it wasn't the fright she'd received but the way he was looking at her so intently that was making her heart pound out of control.

Someone dropped something in an examination cubicle, the clanging noise breaking the moment between them. Beth looked away and glanced down at the notes, trying to figure out what she'd been writing. 'I guess you'll have to learn how to walk more noisily if you don't want to keep giving your staff heart attacks.'

'I guess so.' He took a few steps away. 'I'll head up to clinic. Make sure someone calls when Andrew's out of X-Ray.'

'Right you are, boss.' With that, she began to write again. Ryan watched her for a second before making his legs move. Why, when she called him *boss,* did he feel so…disheartened? Ryan shook his head as he headed to the stairwell and took the stairs two at a time. He was her boss. Why should he feel strange if she called him that?

As he walked into clinic, Tristan nearly applauded. 'About time,' he grumbled. 'Where's Beth?'

'Still in A and E.' Ryan picked up a set of case notes, knowing the only way to get his perky blonde registrar out of his head was to concentrate on work. He headed out into the waiting room to call his first patient through. He managed to see two patients before getting the call to return to A and E to review Andrew's X-rays.

When he walked into A and E, Beth was sitting at the nurses' station, where he'd left her. 'Patient was quick in X-Ray,' he commented.

'The coach tagged along and made Lisa's life miserable so she did Andrew's X-rays immediately.' Beth started taking some out of the packet. 'They haven't been reported on and Lisa said right at this moment she didn't care, so long as the coach and his star player were out of her department.'

Ryan nodded before glancing at the X-rays on the viewer. 'Shoulder is dislocated with what looks like a hairline fracture.'

'The ligaments of the acromioclavicular joint look injured but, thankfully, not completely disrupted. The anterior capsule looks as though it's torn from the anterior surface of the glenoid.'

'Bankart lesion,' Ryan stated. 'Common in hockey players.'

'Do you think it's OK to relocate the shoulder?'

'Yes. Immobilisation of the shoulder should help everything to heal, along with active and passive physio. Scans of the knee?'

Beth changed the radiographs over. 'Medial collateral ligament looks like the winner.'

'Spine?'

She changed the X-rays again. 'Fine. No spinal damage. He still needs to have the ultrasound on his groin area and I'd like to do X-rays of his right thigh.'

'Any reason why?'

Beth frowned a little and took out one of the X-rays of the right knee. 'See here. We only get a little bit of the femur but if you look just at the top here of the X-ray, that doesn't look right.'

They both peered at the radiograph. 'Is it a processing error?' Ryan rubbed the radiograph with his finger.

'I don't know what it is. It looks like the tip of bone in the muscle, which is why I want the X-ray repeated.'

'Good. We need to rule out inflammatory disease of the muscle. The last thing the star hockey player needs is a case of myositis ossificans where his muscles start to grow a new bone for him.'

Beth agreed. 'Wouldn't the coach hit the roof if that was the case!'

'That, and a lot more. It would end Andrew's career.'

'Then it's good that we're checking this out.' She took the X-rays down. 'When do you want to operate?'

Ryan nodded. 'We'll need to relocate that shoulder under general anaesthetic so we may as well get him into Theatre as soon as possible. I'm presuming they want him done privately, so I'll operate and you can assist. Get him started immediately on a course of non-steroidal anti-inflammatories; get him started on heparin for the next twenty-four hours, then review. Anaesthetist and physio reviews as well. What about his pelvis? Do we have views of that?'

Beth quickly looked through the X-ray packet and pulled out a set of X-rays. 'Looks fine. I thought he might have done some damage to his neck of femur but it's looking good.'

Ryan pondered the X-ray for a moment. 'See, this is the top of the femur and there's nothing there. Perhaps it was just an anomaly on that other radiograph.'

'Perhaps.'

'You don't sound convinced.'

'I think it's worth looking into.'

'I totally agree, Beth. Andrew's been lucky to get away with just a shoulder and knee injury. When a hockey player goes into a slide, it can end up a lot worse than we've seen today. He was lucky it was just practice and not a full game.' Ryan shifted away from where he'd been leaning against the desk. 'Which cubicle is he in?'

'Twelve.'

'Right.' He started to walk off, then stopped. 'Er…just out of curiosity. What kept you stuck in A and E? Tristan was annoyed you weren't in clinic.'

'Another orthopaedic review was needed in cubicle five.' She shrugged. 'I was here. I'm the ortho reg on call. Clinic waits. Tris gets more annoyed.'

'Just as well you're good friends.'

'Just as well,' she repeated as she picked up the X-rays. 'Shall we go speak to Andrew?'

'Yes. He'll be glad to take off that cervical collar.'

'If that femur X-ray shows what I think it might show, that wouldn't have been caused by today's slide.'

'No,' Ryan agreed. 'Myositis ossificans can be seen as early as two weeks after a blunt trauma to the thigh but if you think that mark was bone growth, then I'd guess the injury happened about four to six weeks ago.'

'Treated as muscle pain. Rest, ice, compression, elevation.'

'Yes. Where's that team doctor?'

'Dr Smithers?'

'Yes. Talk to him, see what information he has.' Ryan pulled back the curtain around Andrew's bed to find the coach speaking earnestly to his player. 'Sorry to interrupt but you are now cleared to take that cervical collar off,' Ryan told his patient. 'Your spine is fine.'

'I knew it,' the coach said.

'Is Dr Smithers around?' Beth asked.

'Right here,' the doctor said, coming in behind them, a takeaway cup of coffee in his hands. 'Sorry. Have you been looking for me?'

Ryan turned his attention to Andrew. 'Your shoulder and knee took the brunt when you collided with the wall. We're going to get Theatre organised as soon as possible to relocate your shoulder and to get your knee sorted out. You've torn your medial collateral ligament.' Ryan pointed to the area on Andrew's uninjured leg. 'We'll tidy that up and then it's just physio to fix the rest of it. Your shoulder, however, will need to be immobilised for at least three weeks.'

'Three weeks!' Coach blustered.

'I'd figured as much,' Dr Smithers said. 'Bankart lesion?'

Beth was a little surprised but Ryan nodded. 'Seen them before, Dr Smithers?'

'Many times.'

'What's a Bankart?' Andrew asked.

'A Bankart lesion,' Ryan continued, 'is also called a labrum tear, or a very specific tear of the labrum. The shoulder joint has a shallow socket and around the joint is a cuff of cartilage which helps stabilise the area. The cartilage is called a labrum and it's what gives the shoulder its wide range of motion.' He moved his own shoulder around in a circle.

'You've torn that cartilage and therefore the stability of the shoulder joint has been compromised. The part of the labrum you've torn is called the inferior glenoidal labrum. Now, ordinarily, we'd prefer you to have physiotherapy to allow healing to occur slowly. However, as you're a professional athlete, we can repair the tear through arthroscopy.'

'Yeah. That sounds the best.' Andrew nodded.

'Arthroscopy?' the coach asked.

'It's when we examine the joint area using a fine-bore fibre-optic endoscope,' Ryan explained. 'There are only a few incisions of about two centimetres each needed. We can then repair the tear without requiring to make large incisions, making healing more rapid.'

'You'll still need a lot of physio and the shoulder will need to be immobilised for at least the next three weeks,' Beth added.

'So you've said.' Andrew's spirits were plummeting as he realised just what lay ahead of him.

'Also, now that you've torn the labrum, statistically speaking, the chances of dislocating the shoulder again is greater than 80 per cent.' Ryan continued to deliver the bad news.

'It's just like any other injury, Andrew,' Dr Smithers chimed in. 'You've weakened the area, but with proper management you'll be back to playing within the month.'

'And the knee?'

'You'll be weight-bearing on that by tomorrow,' Beth said.

'You're doing the surgery.' Coach pointed at Ryan. 'You're the head of unit. We want this done privately.'

'Of course. However, I'd like to suggest we operate on Andrew here, and once he's out of surgery we can transfer him to a private hospital of your choice.'

The coach named a popular private hospital where elite athletes were often rehabilitated from injury. 'I'll get that organised,' Beth said, after Ryan nodded his consent.

'Dr Smithers will be in Theatre with you,' the coach continued to demand.

'Of course,' Ryan said again. 'Beth?'

'I'm on it,' she said, and headed from the room. She spent the next hour organising further radiographs, specifically of Andrew's right thigh, as well as organising Theatre. When everything was done, she went to find Dr Smithers and found him sitting back in the waiting area of A and E.

'Dr Smithers, would you like to come through?'

The man smiled at her and followed her through to the emergency theatres. 'I'd like to apologise for Coach's behaviour.'

Beth smiled. 'We've handled worse.'

Dr Smithers chuckled. 'I'm sure you have. Sir Ryan is a lot younger than I expected. For some reason, I thought he was older.'

'He's thirty-seven.'

'Has he been at the hospital long?'

'First day on the job—for both of us.' She smiled at him. 'Please, don't tell the coach because I fear the information would upset him.'

Dr Smithers laughed again. 'You're right there, my dear. Oh, I have no doubt as to Sir Ryan's abilities, or yours. I remember reading about Sir Ryan when he was first knighted and he deserved it for the work he did.'

'I've read quite a few of his papers, not only to do with his invention but also the technique he uses for microsurgery,' Beth admitted. 'He's quite brilliant.'

'Have you read his thesis?'

'Not yet but it's on my to-do list.' In fact, she'd meant to do it before she arrived back in Australia but things had been hectic. Now, with Ryan so close, she felt kind of strange reading his work.

'It's really very good.'

Beth smiled and showed Dr Smithers to the changing rooms. Just after she'd changed back into theatre scrubs, her pager beeped. She checked the number. 'Ryan,' she mumbled, and went in search of a phone. 'Hi,' she said when he'd picked up. 'I was just going to call you. Patient is with the anaesthetist, Dr Smithers is ready to go, so we're just waiting on you.'

'I'll be right there.'

Beth went and spoke to Andrew. 'How are you feeling?'

'Drowsy.'

Beth smiled. 'Good.'

'You have such pretty eyes,' Andrew drawled, and Beth's smile increased.

'Thank you.'

'Finished, Dr Durant?' Ryan's voice came from just behind her.

'Almost. Come and talk to Andrew.'

Ryan walked over, standing so close to her his arm brushed against hers. The heat, the immediate awareness of each other stunned them both and Beth quickly shifted back and out of his way.

'Wow,' Andrew said, looking up at Ryan. 'You have pretty eyes, too.'

Beth chuckled. 'Aw-w. Isn't that nice of him to say so?' When Ryan turned to glare at her she shrugged. 'What?'

'Let's get scrubbed.' He stalked out of the room and Beth followed him to the scrub sink. 'It's hardly professional to tease your patients, Dr Durant.'

'I wasn't teasing him. I was teasing you. Big difference. Besides, you do have nice eyes.' Beth shrugged, letting him make of that whatever he wanted.

Dr Smithers walked over to them. 'I've just seen young Andrew and you'll never guess what he said.'

'You have nice eyes?' Beth grinned as dawning realisation crossed Dr Smithers's face.

'Ah. Has he been saying that to everyone?'

'Everyone he's seen since the pre-anaesthetic took effect.'

'Can we concentrate, please?' Ryan growled.

Beth wiped the smile from her face as she continued to scrub. 'Of course, Sir Ryan.' They discussed the operation and exactly what Ryan was planning to do.

'Once the shoulder's done, then we'll move on to the knee. Is all the equipment ready?' he asked Beth.

'Everything's in place, Doctor.'

'What about the X-ray of his right thigh?'

'The films are being reported on but I've had a look at them. It does look as though he has myositis ossificans.'

'Pardon?' Dr Smithers said.

'Did Andrew injure his right thigh about a month or two ago?' Beth asked.

'Er…yes. As far as I can recall. Received a crushing blow with a puck.'

'I thought they were usually all padded up?' she asked.

'It was at a social event. A few of them took to the ice to impress the girls.'

'I'd hardly call a hockey puck in the leg impressive.' Beth frowned.

'Oh, the girls were very impressed the way he took it like a man. I requested X-rays but everything seemed fine. Now he's developed myositis ossificans? I've only seen that once and it was a long time ago.'

'It's quite amazing that a small piece of bone can actually grow within a muscle. Still, it's not where it's supposed to be and we can easily remove it.'

'Will you be doing that now?'

Beth glanced at Ryan. 'I don't see why not,' he said eventually. 'He'll already be having rehabilitation for that leg. Did you discuss the possibility with him, Beth?'

'I discussed everything with him, showed him the X-rays. He was quite astounded. He signed the forms before the pre-med.'

'Good.' Ryan elbowed off the taps. 'Then let's get this show on the road.'

By the time they were finished in Theatre, clinic was well and truly over. Andrew was in Recovery and doing well by all accounts. They'd found no surprises, no hidden complications. She loved it when surgery went smoothly. Dr Smithers was not only happy with the way things had gone but was now a fully paid-up member of the Sir Ryan Cooper fan club.

'You go do what you need to do,' he told Beth. 'I'll deal with Andrew's transfer and fill Coach in on any necessary information.'

'Thank you. I'll call to check on Andrew later.'

'I'd appreciate that. Oh, and thank Sir Ryan again for me. It was a pleasure to watch him work.'

She smiled politely. 'I will.' After she'd changed once more, she told the triage sister she was going out. Although she was still on call for a few more hours, she was determined to have dinner, especially after skipping both breakfast and lunch. She was just walking out of the hospital, her coat pulled around her, her scarf, gloves and hat helping to lock out the cool July wind, when she heard her name being called. She turned and saw Ryan walking briskly towards her.

'Can I speak to you for a moment?'

She was too tired to argue, too tired to evade. 'Only if it's over dinner.'

'Haven't eaten much today?'

'Try nothing…unless coffee is counted.'

Ryan shook his head. 'Where are you headed?'

'Up the street to a nice, quiet Italian restaurant. A high-carb dinner is definitely on the menu.'

'Fine. Let's go.' He placed his hand beneath her elbow and propelled her forward. Beth shrugged from his grasp.

'I'm more than capable of walking by myself, Sir Ryan.' There was no way she could tell him that a simple touch from him sent her insides into a frenzy of sparkles which only made her want him to touch her even more. She had to learn to curb her body's reaction where he was concerned. If she didn't, she'd wind up making a fool of herself and she'd done that in the past too many times where men were concerned.

Beth risked a sidelong glance at Ryan, his face in profile as they walked up the street. The sparkles returned and she realised she had her work cut out for her if she was going to build any antibiodies to fight his natural charm.

CHAPTER THREE

'So,' SHE said as they walked up the street. 'Where were you headed?' He was dressed up for the outdoors, his briefcase in his hand.

'Back to my parents' house. I've been staying with them since I arrived back on Friday. Wow. I can't believe I've only been back in the country for three days.'

'Still jet-lagged?'

'It's almost gone. How about you?'

'I got back on Thursday so I've had an extra day to sleep.'

'When did you start work?'

'Early this morning. Whoever did the roster definitely has a sense of humour. "Let's welcome Beth back by putting her on call on her first day." Yeah. Real funny,' she growled as they continued up the street.

'Where's this restaurant? It's freezing out here.'

Beth laughed. 'We're a pair. Both of us coming from the northern hemisphere summer to the Australian winter.'

'One day sunshine and the next freezing cold. Not fair,' he agreed.

Beth laughed again and the sound warmed him. He wished he knew what it was about this woman that made him react this way because he'd really like to stop it if he could.

'Round the corner and we're there.'

Three minutes later, they'd shed their coats and were seated at a table near the fireplace. Slowly, during dinner, they both thawed out and although the conversation was on general topics, Beth was glad he'd dropped the sir from his personae. Still, she was curious about it.

'So what's it like? Being knighted, I mean?' She stirred her coffee.

'All pomp and ceremony. Kneel, tap on the shoulder.' He shrugged nonchalantly. 'It was nice pomp, but I never asked for it.'

'The knighthood? No. They don't usually hand them out willy-nilly and most certainly never if you ask.' She snapped her fingers in mock disappointment. 'Now I know my mistake. I guess I shouldn't have sent all those emails asking when it was my turn.'

He smiled at her teasing but didn't say any more.

'Come on,' she prompted. 'You can't leave me hanging like that. I've read some of the papers you've written…not your thesis. That's on my to-be-read pile but I mean, what initially inspired you to invent the new technique for microsurgical reattachment of limbs and the instruments to do it with?'

Ryan looked at her for a moment, wondering whether she was really interested in the medical details or whether she was more interested in his knighthood. Since he'd received it, many women, including Geraldine, had thrown themselves at him… and he'd been disgusted. Why couldn't a woman like him for who he was, rather than the medical breakthroughs he'd made? Then again, shouldn't he give Beth the benefit of the doubt? Not all women were like Geraldine.

'Being in the field—'

'A war zone?'

'Yes, or an area where there aren't a lot of medical supplies, you learn to improvise. It's just part and parcel of the job. What I hadn't counted on was the number of amputations. The statistics are about three to one.'

'So every third person has lost part of a limb.' Beth nodded. She'd read his papers, as she'd said, but hearing it from him, the emotion in his tone made everything more real, more tangible and she was right there with him.

'Yes. Most times the only course of action is to amputate the limb and then rehabilitate. It made me wonder whether we couldn't work at reattaching the limbs in some way to save as many limbs as we could, but without the latest equipment and trained staff there didn't seem to be much hope.'

'But you provided that hope.'

'It was an illogical conclusion that worked. Creating a new instrument, which I made by pulling apart several broken ones and blending them together, miraculously worked. The theory was there and I was able to prove the theory correct.'

'What do you mean by an illogical conclusion?'

'It wasn't medically or scientifically possible, but the human body works in mysterious ways and we as doctors only understand a portion of what the vessels we live in are capable of.'

'So your gamble paid off.'

'Basically, yes.'

'And you feel a fraud for receiving a knighthood for that?'

Ryan almost choked on his mouthful of coffee. How could she know that? Did she see it in him? Sense it in him?

'You shouldn't,' she continued. 'Some of the best medical breakthroughs have been discovered by accident. Take penicillin, for example. What matters, Ryan, is that you had the guts to try something different. The fact that it worked is a bonus.'

'Hmm.'

'You like to play down the fact that you've done something brilliant.'

'That's just the point. I haven't done anything brilliant. My only thought was to help other people—most doctors do that. I'd become impatient with the way things were done, devised a new way of doing it and received a knighthood for it. That doesn't seem fair.'

'Fair? I think it's very fair. And what about all those people out there? The ones who are walking around with two legs instead of one because of what you had the guts to try? I'm sure they'd think differently.'

'I'm a doctor, Beth. I help people. That's why I became a doctor. I wanted to help people, to make them better. Isn't that why you became a doctor?'

'Yes, but let's face it, Ryan, some doctors are better than others, regardless of their motivations.'

'Motivations such as money?'

'It's true that some people go into medicine for the money they can make, which, when you think what's involved in obtaining a medical degree, doesn't make sense…well, not to me but you're not one of that type of doctor.'

'You've got that straight.' Ryan drained his coffee and pushed the cup away as a picture of Geraldine flashed through his mind. He could never understand why she'd even pursued medicine as she didn't have a nurturing bone in her body. At first he'd been amused by the way she'd complained about studying all the time and the long hours and, in actual fact, he'd truly believed she'd just been complaining, but somewhere along the line her focus had changed and she'd honestly started hating her job. What she'd liked, though, had been the money and the more she'd made, the more shallow she'd become.

Beth raised her eyebrows at his tone. 'There's more to this than you're telling me.'

'How very astute of you, Dr Durant.'

'Are you going to tell me?'

'I hardly know you.'

'Hello? Isn't talking to someone about your past how you get to know them? Come on, take a chance. Share.'

'Share?'

'Ryan, you don't make comments such as that without having the emotional scars to go with them.'

He thought for a moment before deciding to let Beth in…just a little. 'Her name was Geraldine. More interested in money than helping people.'

'Why did she become a doctor, then?'

'It's what her father wanted.'

Beth remained silent, watching as Ryan looked away, and she

knew he was taking a trip into the past. The question was, would he take her with him?

'She went into neurosurgery.'

'Ah, yes. Money to be made in neurosurgery,' Beth agreed.

'Her father was very wealthy and influential and all her life she'd known she was expected to go into medicine. Even at university, she struggled. It's how we met. She needed a tutor and as I was a year ahead, doing my final year…' He shrugged, as though that made perfect sense. 'We became friends, then started dating and for a while everything was great. She was the one. I was in love and everything seemed set to follow the normal course of action.'

'Then things changed?'

'I graduated, started working and began earning my own money. For some reason, that bothered her. Years later, I realised that even though her father was providing everything she needed, he was also controlling her. To her, making money meant freedom from her father.'

'Hindsight.'

'The problem was, she never seemed to make enough money. Then she turned her sights on me and demanded I do more courses so that I could earn more money.' He shook his head sadly. 'I watched her change and there was nothing I could do about it. I was helpless and then she turned her venom on me.' He shrugged. 'And that's all there was to it…until we met up again a few years back and I made exactly the same mistakes all over again.'

'But she did rip your heart out, didn't she?'

Ryan nodded once and met her gaze. 'Twice.' He exhaled slowly, glad it no longer hurt to discuss his past. It had actually felt good telling Beth about Geraldine, even though he'd revealed a little more than he'd planned. Leaning forward a little, he said, 'And what about you?'

'What about me?'

'Are you a card-carrying member of the "I've had my heart ripped out" club?'

Beth laughed. 'Find me someone who isn't.'

'Is that a yes?'

'That's a yes.'

'Details?'

'He was an A and E registrar. He was very dedicated to his work, a perfectionist, which is great in the professional field but sometimes not so good in private life.' Beth chose her words carefully. 'He had a picture in his head of the perfect life—career, wife, 2.5 children, white picket fence.' She shrugged. 'I thought I'd hit the jackpot. Here was a man who was interested in a life-long commitment and who professed to love me. I was in seventh heaven and then, when it came to crunch time, he…' She swallowed uneasily. 'He decided that I didn't quite fit his perfect picture after all. He left.'

'That's it?'

'More or less.'

'And so your new standard-dating regime was born?'

Beth tried to laugh but it turned into a sigh. 'Basically.'

'Hence the reason so many men seem quite happy you're back at the hospital.'

'I guess, although now I'm not interested in it any more. America was good for me. It let me get away, start a clean slate in some respects.'

'Did you speed-date there?'

'No, and now that I'm back, as I said, I'm just not interested in trying to find Mr Right.'

'That's a pity.'

Beth felt tingles ripple over her skin at his words and her mouth went dry. She swallowed. 'It is?'

'Yes.'

'Why?'

His gaze intensified and he lowered his voice. 'Because there's this amazing chemistry between us, Beth. It was there the first time we met at the Christmas dinner you organised.'

'I didn't organise it. I suggested it. Big difference. Besides, you were mean to me.'

'I was annoyed with you.'

'Why?'

'Because you were having more fun than I was.'

She laughed incredulously. 'What? When?'

'When boring old Richard was making his speech. You and Tristan were sharing your own private joke.'

Beth thought back and nodded. 'Yes, we were. So that's what made you narky.'

'I wasn't…narky—whatever that means.'

'It means getting your nose out of joint.'

He thought for a moment. 'Well, in that case, yes, I was.' He reached out and took her hand in his and the warmth immediately spread up her arm and exploded throughout her body. 'You looked incredible. That dress you wore…' He shook his head and closed his eyes for a moment, a vision of Beth dressed in the shimmering burgundy outfit coming easily to his mind. Ryan opened his eyes. 'And there you were, looking amazing and sexy and sharing a joke with Tristan.'

'But we're just friends.'

'I didn't know that then.'

'So you got narky.'

'I did. It's still there, Beth.'

'The narkiness?' She smiled.

'The attraction,' he clarified firmly.

She sighed again. 'I know.'

'Yet neither of us likes to date colleagues and we've both had our hearts ripped out in the past.'

'Which makes it almost impossible for us to take a step out in faith and trust someone else with them.'

'Correct. So what do we do?'

Beth thought for a moment and reluctantly removed her hand from his. 'It's easy. You look for another job and we both see a cardiologist.'

Ryan stared at her for a long moment before he realised she was using dry humour as a cover-up. 'You're sassing me, right?'

She smiled. 'Duh.'

'Duh? You were in America too long.'

Beth was glad they seemed to be back on a more level footing, the tension easing between them. 'But I'm glad to be home.'

'Sydney's home for you?'

'Yep. I'm a Sydney girl. My parents live here but they're travelling at the moment.'

'Are you staying in their house?'

'No. They've been travelling for the past four months so they rented their house out. At the moment, I'm at the hotel with Natalie.'

'Ah, of course. All the wedding preparations and bridesmaid's duties to do.'

'Oh.' She hit herself in the head. 'You're the best man, aren't you? How could I have forgotten that?'

'I have no idea, but I do know one of my main responsibilities for the entire ceremony is to look after the bridesmaid.'

'Oh? Well…that would be me.'

Ryan didn't reply but smiled at her, the smile that made her heartbeat increase, her palms perspire and her body turn to a mass of jelly. Her gaze meshed with his and the tension levels tripled from what they'd been before. The blue of his eyes was dark and intense, even more so in the flickering firelight. She swallowed, realising this thing between them was moving along a lot faster than she'd anticipated and soon she would have Ryan all to herself at the wedding.

Did she want that?

Of course, came the immediate answer, but only if he stayed as he was now, relaxed and happy. It was bad enough trying to deal with his mercurial moods at the hospital, she didn't want to have to worry about that on Natalie and Marty's big day. Then again, when he was in 'Sir Ryan' mode, he was less irresistible and charming and more annoying and frustrating.

Either way, she'd already discovered she wasn't as immune to him as she'd thought, in which case, did she have any hope of survival?

CHAPTER FOUR

'THAT was a fantastic wedding,' Ryan said to the groom as they lazed back against the bar.

Marty smiled. 'It sure was.' They both looked across the room to where Natalie was laughing with Beth. While Marty only had eyes for his wife, Ryan couldn't take his eyes off Beth. They'd had a great time all day long and he'd been more than happy to look after her as part of his best man duties. Right now she was laughing wholeheartedly at something Natalie had said, and she looked incredible.

His gut started to twist and he forced himself to look away. 'You're a lucky man, Marty,' he said, slapping his cousin on the back.

'You can say that again. Married to my best friend.'

'I thought I'd never see the day you settled down.'

'It's easy with the right woman and my darling Nat is so perfect for me.' Marty reluctantly pulled his attention away from his new wife to look at Ryan. 'Now we just need to get you sorted out.'

Ryan held up both hands. 'No way. No, thank you. I'm more than happy being single.'

'Taking over my mantle as eligible bachelor at St Gregory's, eh?'

Ryan chuckled. 'Mantle? What mantle? You arrived, saw Natalie and that was it.'

'True but, still, you fit the bill nicely. You're successful, you're good-looking, you're—'

'Making me blush,' Ryan finished, wanting to glance back over at Beth but forcing himself not to. 'I don't have time for dating and, besides, I've discovered in the past that a lot of women are more impressed by the title than by me.'

'A lot of women, eh?' Marty laughed. 'I've missed your ego, Ry, and of course you have loads of time to have a private life. As Sir Ryan, you have two secretaries, registrars, interns and a partridge in a pear tree to do your bidding.'

Ryan shifted uneasily at the mention of his title. Even though it had been over a year since he'd received the accolade, he still wasn't comfortable with it. Now he was back in Australia after years of living both in London and elsewhere overseas. During the next six months he would be teaching the new technique he'd developed to all orthopaedic registrars and surgeons, not only in Sydney but in the rest of Australia as well. It was no wonder he needed two secretaries.

Realising his cousin was waiting for an answer, Ryan merely laughed. 'It's good to be back home. I've really missed you, Marty.' He ruffled his friend's hair, as he'd done when they'd been kids. Both of them were only children and had been raised more as brothers than cousins. 'So, are you going to hand over the keys?'

'What? Don't you want to continue staying with your folks?'

Ryan shook his head. 'I love my parents dearly but I'm also a big boy now and very used to my own space. So hand them over!'

'All right, all right.' Marty fished in his tuxedo trousers and pulled out a set of keys. 'Thanks for volunteering to look after the house while we're on our honeymoon.'

'Thanks for giving me a car to drive and a place to crash until I can get set up.'

'Just don't drive the house and crash the car,' Marty joked.

'Funny. How long will you be gone?'

'Three weeks. Three glorious weeks with my beautiful bride in sunny Fiji, so make sure you're out of the house by then.'

'Will do. Escaping the Australian winter?' Ryan shook his head as he watched Marty once more glance at his new wife. If looks could devour… 'While I get stuck in winter forever.'

Marty laughed but didn't look at him. 'Surely the Australian winter isn't a patch on the London winter.'

'True, but it's still cold. I'll be glad when spring comes.' He realised Marty wasn't paying him the slightest bit of attention as Natalie was walking towards them...or rather she was walking towards her new husband, the love-birds only having eyes for each other. She went willingly into Marty's arms as though she belonged there, and for a moment Ryan felt a pang of envy. Would a woman ever look at him in that adoring way? Would she feel totally at home with his arms wrapped around her? Was that what he wanted?

He watched as Natalie accepted the kisses from her husband, before turning to smile at her new cousin-in-law. Ryan could just see the faint outline of Natalie's scars beneath her make-up. Six months ago she'd received burns to her right arm and a few minor burns to her face after saving a child from a burning building. Now, though, only those with a trained eye would notice the scars. Indeed, the range of movement in her arm was remarkable and the scarring minimal. She'd been very lucky, but perhaps it had been pure love which had got her through the worst of her ordeal.

'Ryan,' she was saying, and he focused his attention on her words. 'Thank you so much for everything.' Natalie leaned forward and kissed him on the cheek. 'Especially the way you've carefully looked after Beth,' she said softly in his ear. 'So attentive.'

Ryan pulled back, not sure what to say. Was it that obvious that he found Beth desirable? Out the corner of his eye he saw the woman in question heading in their direction, the swish of silk moving in time with her gorgeous body. Beth really did look amazing in the deep red of her dress. It had certainly been made to fit her and was an off-the-shoulder style, revealing a generous amount of neck which begged to be nuzzled. A few tendrils of her blonde hair hung down to tantalise him even more, and the small roses adorning her hair like a crown suited her perfectly.

When he met her gaze, he took in the tiredness of her brown eyes, even though they still twinkled with laughter. He found himself reaching for her hand and lacing his fingers with hers. 'Can your feet stand one more dance?' He leaned a little closer and whispered, 'There's no point even trying to have a conversation with these two. They're way too mushy.'

Beth smiled, unable to stop the jolt of tingles that spread up her arm at Ryan's touch. It had happened every single time he'd touched her today and as he'd been responsible for escorting her and standing next to her in photographs and dancing with her and making sure she had everything she needed…the tingles had almost become permanent.

'OK, but this is the last dance because I'm really starting to get worn out.'

'It has been exhausting.' They made their way onto the dance floor. As soon as they arrived, the music changed to a slow number and Ryan was glad of the opportunity to pull Beth into his arms. She felt nice there.

They both swayed in time with the music, Beth fighting hard against fatigue to hold herself in check. She couldn't let today's events get to her. Ryan had been marvellous and wonderful and deliciously sexy and funny, but she knew she had to resist him because today was just a bubble in time. Tomorrow they would go back to being colleagues and she *had* to keep her head.

'How much longer until you're qualified?'

The question startled her a little. They'd talked of many topics throughout the day but this was the first time he'd mentioned work, and as she looked up at him she realised the bubble was starting to burst. She forced a polite smile.

'I'm in the home stretch. I have my final oral exam in October and then in February next year I'm qualified.'

'Looking forward to it?'

'Definitely.'

'Private practice?'

Beth hesitated. 'I'm not sure. I'm still weighing my options.'

'That's wise. If you want to discuss your career at any time, let me know.'

Beth was a little surprised at the offer. 'Thanks.'

'You're more than welcome.' He smiled down at her but as their gazes continued to hold, the smile slipped from his face and his blue eyes became more serious. She became more aware of his hands at her back, the feel of their bodies, so close yet so far apart. There was a warmth…a sensual warmth, emanating from him and winding itself around her. She went willingly, allowing him to break the gaze and draw her closer. She rested her head on his shoulder, breathing in the electrifying scent of him. She'd hoped it would wake her up a little but instead it seemed to subdue her inhibitions so that when Ryan led her off the dance floor to a secluded corner of the room, she went willingly.

They sat down at a deserted table as almost everyone else was on the dance floor, enjoying the last few songs.

'Have you had a good night so far?' Ryan asked, his gaze never leaving Beth's. He shifted his chair closer, leaning one arm on the table and resting his head in his hand. He was giving her his undivided attention and he wanted to make sure she realised it.

'It's been wonderful.' Beth was captivated by him.

'I'm glad you've enjoyed it.' His voice was deep, intense, and both knew they were having two separate conversations. The one they were having with their bodies seemed much more interesting but also risky at the same time. Still, she liked playing with fire.

'How about you?'

'Terrific.'

Silence. They continued the conversation without words for a few moments before Ryan whispered, 'Come closer, Beth.'

She shifted in her chair, angling closer, her gaze flicking between his mouth and his eyes. The bubble around them was becoming more intense, more potent with an attraction they both felt. She held back a little, wanting him to do a bit of work towards what would eventually happen.

'Closer,' he continued.

She shifted slightly but still not enough.

'OK. I'll move,' he murmured, leaning towards her, his lips a hair's breadth from her own. 'How's that?'

'Mmm. Better,' she returned, her voice husky. Her eyelids fluttered closed and she breathed in, waiting with anticipation for his lips to be on hers.

'Ryan?' Where's Ryan?' came a call from the groom.

Ryan sprang up out of his chair, overturning it in his hurry. He was around the table and heading into the crowd before Beth had time to breathe out. 'What?' She tried to follow his progress as he mingled with the people on the dance floor. Everyone was standing still, looking expectantly for Ryan. It was then Beth realised the band had stopped playing. Their final set was over but the groom, before he left, was demanding one more song…one song from Ryan.

'Ryan?' Beth muttered as she stood, her legs a little wobbly, and made her way over to the edge of the dance floor. Sure enough, Ryan was taking his seat behind the piano, while Marty dragged over a microphone. 'He can play?' she said out loud.

'You bet he can play,' Natalie said, and Beth turned to find her friend watching her closely.

'Really?' Beth looked from her friend and back to the man in question, who was beginning to tinkle the ivories. 'He told me he liked jazz but I had no idea he could play.'

'Oh, yeah. Marty said Ryan could have been a professional musician if he hadn't been so dedicated to medicine.' Natalie stood beside her as they listened to Ryan begin to play the song Marty had requested. His voice was smooth and deep and washed over Beth like the silk of her dress, only this was making her feel soft and sexy on the inside while the fabric made her feel that way on the outside.

A few times during the song he glanced in her direction and although she wanted to look away, feeling slightly embarrassed, she couldn't. His voice continued to warm her and she was mesmerised until he'd finished the song and everyone clapped. Next, Marty persuaded him to play a more lively, jazzy tune about unrequited love, the song making fun of the act.

'I'm sorry about before,' Natalie murmured.

Beth looked at her and frowned. 'What "before"?'

'When you and Ryan were all cosy in the corner. I didn't realise Marty was going to call him over or I would never have let
him interrupt the two of you.'

Beth felt the colour drain from her. 'You saw?' She swallowed, not sure how she felt.

'Hey, I think it's good. You and Ryan are cute together.'

Beth recovered a moment later, deciding to play it nice and
easy…on the surface, anyway…rather than confide in Natalie
just how much Ryan had rocked her world in such a short time.
The man, it seemed, was perfect, and that in itself made her a little nervous. She was used to meeting a guy, asking a set of pre-
defined questions, and if their answers didn't match up with
what she was looking for, then after one or two dates, she sent
them on their way.

The reason she'd created the questions was to find a man
willing to take the same risks she was willing to take. A man who
had the same sense of values she did. There was a lot at stake—
her future happiness—and she needed to make careful choices
if she was going to be successful.

Of course, there had to be chemistry as well. Chemistry between
herself and a man was vitally important. Sometimes she found it
but didn't get the answers she liked and other times vice versa.

'There seemed to be good chemistry between the two of you
tonight,' Natalie said, obviously reading her friend's mind. 'But,
please, tell me, was he helping you get something out of your
eye or was he about to kiss you because your faces were awfully
close?'

'Uh…' Beth floundered and Natalie laughed.

'The latter, eh? Glad to hear it. Ryan's a great guy.'

'Hmm.' Beth had managed to recover some of her composure.

'So has this been going on long? After all, you've had a whole
week working together at the hospital.'

'Well…I'm attracted.'

'And so is he, by the look of things, but when did it start?
Monday? Tuesday?'

'Try Christmas.'

'What?' Natalie gaped at her friend.

'Well, nothing really happened. We shared a couple of goofy looks, we shared a moment, we exchanged harsh words…' Beth shrugged. 'You know, the basics.'

'You didn't say anything.'

'You had your hands full with your own problems if you recall.'

Natalie nodded. 'So did you think about him when you were in America?'

'Now and then.'

'And still you didn't say anything?'

'What was I supposed to say? I had no idea what was going on.'

Natalie smiled at her friend and placed a hand on her arm. 'Hey, I'm not picking on you, honey. I just hadn't realised you were attracted to him back then. In fact, all week long you've been closed every time I've mentioned Ryan yet today…today has shown that there's definitely something between you both. Do you want to talk about it? Do I need to help you in any way?'

'Don't worry about me.' Beth took Natalie's hand in hers and gave it a quick squeeze before letting go. 'I'm fine and the reason I didn't say anything about work was there's nothing to say.' She frowned for a moment. 'Ryan's rather different at work.'

'I guess he has to be. Lots of responsibility.'

'His choice.'

Natalie looked over to where Ryan had started another number. 'Is it?' They were quiet for a few minutes before she asked, 'So does his good behaviour today mean he gets a second date with you?'

'Second date? When was the first?'

'Today.'

'This wasn't a date, Natalie. This was your wedding where you and Marty threw us together. The poor man has been saddled with his "looking after the bridesmaid" duties all day and well into the evening, too.'

'What a hardship,' Natalie joked. 'Yet I don't hear either of you complaining. In fact, I'd say Ryan has been enjoying himself immensely. He was certainly holding you close on the dance floor.'

'Hey, what is this? You're supposed to be totally wrapped up in your husband.'

'I am.'

'Then why are you spying on me?'

'I'm not spying. I'm merely paying attention to what my guests are doing. That's one of the bride's responsibilities and I take my bridal responsibilities very seriously.'

'Anyway, things will be different at work on Monday,' Beth said softly, her words holding a hint of sadness.

They both were silent for a moment, listening to the music. A woman had joined Ryan at the piano and the two were playing a funky duet, Ryan's voice still ringing out clear and true. Beth didn't like the look of the woman sitting beside him, or the way she was squashed up against Ryan, so she turned away. 'Is there something I'm supposed to be helping you with? Do you need your make-up fixed? Your hair re-pinned? Anything? After all, I'm the bridesmaid and as Ryan has done his duty tonight, I also need to keep doing mine and that is to assist the bride at all times…except when she leaves with her new husband. Then you're on your own.'

Natalie laughed. 'I should hope so. I can't think of anything I need help with at the moment. Oh, except for you to pass on to your parents how much I've missed them tonight. It's such a pity they couldn't be here.'

'I know. Mum was really sorry to miss it but they booked their tour of Alaska so long ago.'

'It must have been good to see them during your time in America.'

'Oh, yes. It was wonderful.'

'When are they back?'

'Few more weeks.' Beth looked at her friend's glowing, radiant face. 'You're so happy,' she said softly.

'Yes. I am.'

'I wish I was as happy as you.'

Natalie hugged Beth. 'You will be. You'll find the right guy. In fact, Ryan has a lot of the same qualities as Marty and the chemistry's there between you, so why not go for it?'

Beth laughed. 'Are you ever going to give up on this idea?'

'Hey, it's a good idea and good ideas are worth pursuing. Look at me. I'm married to my best friend, whom I love with all my heart, and on top of that my doctor has cleared me to go back to work after the honeymoon.'

'Really?' Beth hugged her friend close.

'I can't wait to get back to work. Although I've been in the paediatric ward, helping out, it's been frustrating not being able to have the authority to do anything.'

'Well, enjoy your honeymoon first and tell Marty not to worry about his house. It'll be in safe hands until you get back.'

'Thanks for agreeing to house-sit. I felt horrible when I had to give up the lease on the unit while you were away but I just couldn't—'

'Stop apologising, Natalie. I told you at the time it was OK. Now, I get to stay at your and Marty's house for three weeks, rent-free, while I look around for something closer to the hospital.'

'I did give you the keys, didn't I?'

'Yes. They're in my bag. Relax and enjoy yourself. That's all I ask.'

Natalie looked at her husband who was making his way over to them. 'I can definitely do that.'

'Mind if I steal her away?' Marty asked, and Beth shook her head. Within another second she was alone, standing on the edge of the dance floor, while people moved and grooved to Ryan's expert jazz. It wouldn't be long until the bride and groom left and then she could get a taxi back to their house and crash. She wondered if she'd have the energy to take off her dress or whether she'd just lie on the bed and close her eyes.

First of all, though, she needed to get out of here. Being a Saturday night in Sydney, it would probably be best if she called and ordered a taxi. She started to make her way through the throng to the table where her bag was.

She heard Ryan announce the next song to be his last and again he made it another lively number. Thankfully, this time the other female pianist had stepped down to let him hog the limelight one last time—which he appeared to be very good at. He had an enigmatic presence, which women of all ages were drawn to, and, much to her chagrin, she found she wasn't immune.

Beth would have swayed along with the music if she hadn't been so tired and her feet so sore. In fact, she was surprised her feet had lasted this long in the high-heeled shoes she wasn't accustomed to wearing, but she knew once she took the shoes off, there was no way she was getting them back on again.

'Another reason to get out of here as soon as Marty and Natalie leave.' She reached into her bag for her phone and ordered a cab, one finger stuck in her other ear so she could hear properly.

As Ryan finished the number, Natalie came over and gave Beth a hug and kiss goodbye. 'Thanks for everything.'

'You are more than welcome.'

Marty wasn't far behind his wife in offering his thanks, and she hugged him, too. 'You're a good friend, Beth.'

'I'm glad you've finally got what you wanted.' They both turned and smiled at Natalie. 'And now go, have a fantastic honeymoon and don't bother sending me a postcard.'

Everyone gathered around to see the happy couple off, and from the safety of the limousine Marty looked at Natalie and smiled. 'Did you see Beth and Ryan?' he asked.

'You interrupted them a moment too soon,' Natalie chided.

'No, I didn't. Now they're both going to be wondering what the kiss would have been like and you and I both know, Mrs Williams, just how much fun curiosity can be.' He kissed his wife. 'At least with them both house-sitting for us, they'll have the opportunity to find out.'

'I still feel guilty about that. We shouldn't be matchmaking. What if it turns out wrong?'

'They'll both forgive us in time and, besides, who says we're matchmaking? We're just giving two people we care about a nudge in the right direction.'

Natalie smiled and shook her head. 'You are bad, my darling husband.'

'Don't I know it,' he murmured as he gathered her close for a long and lasting kiss.

Back at the reception, Beth watched as a taxi pulled into the venue's driveway and went over to check it was the one she'd ordered. It was. 'I'll just get my bag and coat. Be right out,' she told the driver, and headed back inside. Now that she'd realised her feet were sore, every step she took grew more painful and her wish to have the shoes off her feet was intensifying.

'Hi, there.' Ryan seemed to come out of nowhere yet suddenly he was close beside her. 'Ready to keep on partying?'

Beth laughed and shook her head. 'Sorry. This bridesmaid has fulfilled all her duties and is now going to take her shoes off and leave.'

'Can I get you a taxi?'

'I've got one waiting.'

'Good. Mind if I share? You may have completed your wedding responsibilities but mine is to look after the bridesmaid, which includes seeing her safely to her place of residence.' He helped her into her coat as proof that he took his responsibilities seriously.

'Ryan. You don't need to go that far.'

'Yes, I do. Marty would shoot me if he thought I'd been lax in my responsibilities. Just let me check everything's under control, say goodbye to my folks and then we can go.'

As quickly as he'd appeared, he disappeared and Beth sighed, not wanting him to share her taxi but also not wanting to fight him on the issue. She just didn't have the mental strength. She started walking towards the door, trying not to grimace with each step. 'Almost there,' she whispered to herself.

'Pardon?' Ryan was back and looked down at her feet. 'Sore?'

'Very.'

'Is that why you weren't up dancing while I was playing?'

'A bit hard to dance when your feet are sore,' she replied, still walking slowly towards the door. 'I'm just tired.' She wasn't going to tell him she hadn't wanted to join the throng of adoring women watching him.

'Why don't you take the shoes off?'

'I intend to, but not here.'

Ryan shook his head and within the next instant had whisked her off her feet. She gasped in surprise and her heart pounded erratically. Was it from fright or the nearness of their bodies? Ryan received a few whistles and calls of encouragement from people around them as he carried her outside to the waiting taxi. Beth felt herself blush and buried her head in Ryan's shoulder, which was a huge mistake as his intoxicating scent once more wound itself around her.

It should be considered dangerous for a man to smell as good as he did and it made her wonder just what would have happened if his lips had met hers earlier. Did he taste just as good? She was sure he would but now wasn't at all certain she wanted to find out. Come Monday, the man would go back to being Sir Ryan again and she wasn't sure it was wise to pursue anything with him, even if it was just a few curious kisses.

As he released her, gently placing her on the ground by the door of the taxi, Beth slid down his tall frame, feeling the firmness of his body against her own. A new wave of longing washed over her and as she glanced up to look at him, she realised they were both on the same page. Both had the same sense of longing and need mixed with a healthy dose of curiosity.

'Ready, miss?' the taxi driver asked.

Once more they had been interrupted on the verge of finding out exactly what it was that existed between them. Ryan held the door for Beth as she climbed in, glad to be off her feet. Ryan climbed into the back seat beside her.

'Where to?' the driver asked.

Beth put her seat belt on, gave Marty's address and the man sped off.

'Where are you going?' Ryan's tone was cautious.

'Marty's house. Natalie asked me to house-sit while they were away on honeymoon.'

'Oh, did she?' Ryan clipped his seat belt into place and shifted in his seat to look at her.

'Why?'

Ryan dug into his trouser pocket and pulled out a set of keys. 'Guess where I'm staying.'

Realisation dawned on Beth, shock and anger flooding through her. 'Natalie!' she growled softly.

'*And* her conniving husband. Trying to matchmake us, are they?'

'It would appear so.'

'It's all right. You stay in the house, I can keep on staying at my parents' house.'

'No. You stay there. I can stay in the hotel for a bit longer until I can find a place to live.'

'I'm in the same boat. No home, no car.'

'How have you been getting to work all week long?'

'Borrowed either my dad's or my mum's car. Honestly, it made me feel like a teenager again, begging for the keys to the car.' He paused and looked at her thoughtfully. 'Then again…Marty's house is quite roomy and there's no reason why we couldn't share.'

'Share?'

'We can both house-sit, can't we? There's two bathrooms, one off the main bedroom and the other at the opposite end of the house.'

'Are you listening to what you're saying? The hospital grapevine would have a field day and although you may be happy with all the attention, I'm not.'

'Why should it matter to the grapevine? We're colleagues and it's only temporary. Three weeks and then we need to move out. Besides, I'll be away some of the time as I'm lecturing interstate. We'll both be looking for new accommodation and working. I can get my secretary to schedule us on for different shifts so we don't need to even see each other. If that's what you want,' he added with a lopsided smile that melted her heart. With her mind being so tired, what he was saying actually made sense and it would be so easy to agree. 'Anyway, think about it, sleep on it. I can stay at my parents' house tonight and we can organise everything tomorrow…when your feet aren't so tired.'

Beth laughed. 'I like the way you assume my feet are heavily involved in my decision-making processes.'

'Aren't they?'

'Not in this instance. You're right. I'm tired. Where are
your bags?'

'At Marty's.'

'Mine, too. I had them sent over from the hotel earlier today.'

In the next instant the taxi driver braked hard and swerved,
honking his horn. Beth and Ryan quickly peered out the window.
The driver had narrowly missed hitting a young woman who was
standing in the middle of the road, looking dazed. A second later,
another screech of brakes was heard from behind them...then a
sickening thud followed by the sound of broken glass.

'She's been hit!'

CHAPTER FIVE

'STOP the car,' Ryan ordered, and both he and Beth had their seat belts off and were exiting the taxi as soon as it was safe to do so. Ryan raced off towards the person who'd been hit.

'Call an ambulance,' Beth told the driver. 'And control the traffic.'

'I've got a first-aid kit in the back,' the driver said. 'Are you both medically trained?'

'Yes,' she replied, and waited impatiently as the taxi driver retrieved his medical kit. She shrugged off her coat, tossing it into the back seat of the car. 'Thanks,' she said when the driver gave her the kit.

'Arnold's my name. I'm trained in first aid if you need any help.'

'We'll let you know.' She rushed over to where Ryan was already beside the pedestrian. The driver of the car that had hit her got out of her vehicle, looking as white as a sheet, protesting that she hadn't seen the woman until it had been too late.

Glad she was still wearing her shoes, Beth picked her way through the debris before kneeling on the opposite side to Ryan. She unzipped the first-aid kit and took out some bandages. 'What have we got?'

'Patient is unconscious, airway is clear but breathing is shallow. Carotid pulse is weakening. Have we got anything to stop this bleeding from her head?'

'Here.' Beth handed him a padded bandage as well as a crêpe bandage to help keep it in place.

'Check her chest.'

Beth felt the woman's ribs, glad for the moment their patient was unconscious. 'Left T4 and 5 feel broken.'

'Pneumothorax?'

'Possibility of it happening but without a stethoscope, I can't tell.' She carefully checked the woman's limbs, which were at odd angles.

'Can you hear me?' Ryan called, and bent down to check the woman's airway again. 'Do we have a penlight torch, or any torch for that matter?'

'Here's one,' Arnold said from behind them. Ryan merely held out his hand, and as soon as he had the torch he checked the woman's eyes.

'Pupils equal and reacting to light. At least that's something. Ambulance?'

'It's on its way and I've got a few other people to stop and help with the traffic,' Arnold reported.

'Thanks, Arnold,' Beth replied, not looking up from her work. 'Fractures to both lower arms. Left upper arm looks bad—scapular fracture. Both lower legs look fractured.'

'Femur?' Ryan asked.

'Both feel fine. Patient has voided.'

'Internal injuries.' Ryan had his fingers pressed to the woman's carotid pulse. 'No!' He leaned down further to listen for breathing sounds. 'She's stopped,' he said.

Behind them, a woman started crying and Beth glanced up to see the driver of the car, her eyes wide with shock, her hands clenched near her face. Beth looked at Arnold. 'Can you…?'

'I'm on it,' Arnold said, and whisked the sobbing woman away.

Beth immediately shifted over and placed her hands on their patient's chest, ready for cardiopulmonary resuscitation, while Ryan placed a thin handkerchief over the woman's lips before pinching her nose and tilting her head back. He breathed five clear breaths into her mouth before Beth began chest compressions.

They continued with their job, Beth counting the compressions out loud until Ryan called that the carotid pulse was back.

She breathed a sigh of relief and sat back for a moment. The wailing sirens in the distance were a most welcome sound.

'I'll go get our ambo friends to join us,' Beth said.

'Good idea,' he murmured, checking the patient's pupils again. The woman groaned and Ryan immediately called to her. 'Can you hear me? What's your name?'

'Ow-w,' the woman whimpered, grimacing in pain.

'It's all right. Help is here,' Ryan said, but received no response. 'She's out again.'

Beth nodded as she stood and walked over to where the ambulance was getting as close as possible to the accident site.

'Hey, Charles,' she said, as one of the paramedics climbed out of the ambulance and walked over.

'Beth! I heard you were back.' Charles came over and kissed Beth's cheek. 'Good to see you.' He continued opening the back of the ambulance to get out what they needed. 'Back for Natalie and Marty's wedding, eh? Nice dress.'

Beth looked down at her dress and saw the dirt on it, especially around the hem. 'Let's hope this stuff washes out.'

'So what have you got for me?' Charles and his partner began to get the stretcher out.

'Female, early twenties. Wandered out into the middle of the road and was struck in the abdomen. Possible pelvic fracture. Fractures to both tibiae, both radius and ulnae, left scapula, left T4 and 5 ribs and skull fracture. Temporary myocardial infarction but was resuscitated and is breathing normally. Regained consciousness for a few seconds after resuscitation but I'd say, due to the pain, she's unconscious again. No signs of Medic-Alert information. Give me an IV line, plasma if you have it. She'll need a transfusion once she reaches the hospital. Draw up 20 micrograms of morphine and I'll administer. Stethoscope?'

'You've got it. Wow. I can't believe you're back,' Charles said as he found what she'd requested, leaving it to his partner to take the stretcher over to the patient.

'Got any gloves in there, mate?' Ryan asked from behind her, and Beth nearly jumped a mile.

'Sure. You want a pair, too, Beth?' He handed some over before drawing up the analgesic Beth had asked for. She hung the stethoscope around her neck, took the syringe and swab and glanced at Ryan. A frown pinched his brow and she wondered whether he was concentrating or whether he'd heard Charles's comment. She shrugged, deciding now was not the time to wonder what Ryan was thinking.

She walked off, leaving Charles to introduce himself to Ryan. Then she heard Charles's laugh of surprise when he realised exactly who Ryan was—the new ortho boss. Bending down, she listened to the woman's chest, glad to hear her lungs weren't rasping. She administered the morphine and a moment later Charles came over to assist his partner in transferring the patient to the stretcher.

'Cervical collar. Pat-slide and lift on three,' Ryan ordered, and when they were ready they each grabbed a handle on the pat-slide and transferred the patient over. Charles raised the stretcher and wheeled it over to the ambulance where they set about inserting an IV cannula.

'You coming with us, Beth?' Charles asked.

'Hey, I'm not on call, Tristan is. Why should we have all the fun? Besides, I think you guys can handle it from here. The patient is stabilised.'

'Sure. So you're gonna stay with Sir Ryan, eh? I forgot he was Marty's cousin. Best man, was he?'

'Yes.'

'I'll bet Natalie looked beautiful.' Charles held out a clipboard to Beth. She quickly scanned the forms, wrote a few lines herself then signed.

'She was gorgeous. Hey, can I keep this stethoscope and scrounge a medical torch, please? I want to check out the driver of the car.'

'No problem.' He handed over the instruments.

'Got a spare sphygmo?'

'Oh, all right, but only because it's you.'

Beth smiled as she accepted the sphygmomanometer so she could check the patient's blood pressure.

'All righty, then, we'll leave you to it.' Charles closed the doors to the ambulance, leaving his partner to attend to the patient. The sound of more sirens filled the air. 'That'll be the cops. You'd better go.' He put one hand on her shoulder and as the warmth of his hand seeped through her dress, it was only then she realised how cold she was. 'Do you want another ambulance for the driver?'

'Might be best. Delayed shock may set in at any moment.' Beth glanced across to where the driver was sitting in the back of Arnold's taxi.

'All right. I'll call it in.'

'Thanks, Charles.' Beth watched as he headed around to the driver's side and climbed in. A moment later, the engine roared to life and the flashing lights came on.

'Beth?' The call came from Ryan and she headed over to the rear of the taxi where he stood waiting for her. Her professional self was starting to slip and the pain she'd ignored in her feet began to return.

'You're not going with the ambulance?' Ryan began to frown. 'Is that responsible?'

Beth glared at him and held up her hand to stop him.

'Don't pull your "Sir Ryan" act with me now. I'm too tired and too cold to care. The patient will be fine until she gets to hospital.'

'Sir Ryan act?' He raised his eyebrows and shoved his hands into his trouser pockets. Even standing there in his tuxedo, in the darkness of night, looking at her in disbelief, he was still incredibly sexy and Beth found it difficult to control her thoughts.

'What?' she asked.

'What do you mean by that?'

'I'm not getting into it now and I still have a patient to review.' She put the instruments down on the boot of Arnold's taxi and rubbed her arms. The action seemed to break his mood and he swivelled round and walked away. Beth closed her eyes for a moment, wondering if things were going to continue to slide. At the sound of footsteps next to her, she opened her eyes again, only to see Ryan standing there, his coat in his hands, holding it out for her.

'Now that the adrenaline rush is over, you'll keep getting colder.'

Beth watched him for a brief moment, trying to figure him out before gratefully sliding her arms into the warm coat.

'Thank you.' The warmth from the coat combined with the nearness of his body helped to raise her falling temperature. She swallowed over the lump in her throat, conscious that his hands stayed on her arms for a split second longer than they should have. Again, she had to force herself to concentrate and hesitantly raised her gaze to meet his. 'I'd better go see to the…other patient.'

'OK. Arnold's been forcing her to drink some sugary tea he had in his taxi.'

'Good.'

'You check out our next patient and I'll go speak to the police. And, look, here's the tow truck.'

Beth collected the instruments and went around the taxi to where the woman sat. 'Hi. I'm Beth. What's your name?'

'Carla.'

'How are you holding up?'

Carla shook her head in disbelief. 'She just came out of nowhere.'

'I know.' Beth sympathised. 'Our taxi almost hit her.'

'Do you know who she is?'

'She didn't regain consciousness long enough for us to ask.'

'Will she die?'

'Her injuries are quite bad.'

'What happens then? I mean, to me? It was an accident. I didn't mean to hit her.'

'It's all right. The police are here and they'll be able to tell you what happens next. I'd like you to go to the hospital, at least overnight, so we can keep an eye on you.'

'But I'm fine.'

'You might feel fine but what's just happened is quite stressful and I, for one, would feel better if you were monitored, at least overnight.'

'How do I get there? My car's wrecked. Do I need to go in an ambulance?'

'I've got one coming for you. Would you like to call a family member or friend to come and help?'

'I've already done that. They're on their way but they might take a while getting through the traffic that's banked up.'

'But they're coming, so that's good.' Beth put her hand reassuringly on Carla's shoulder. 'Everything will get sorted out but sometimes it does take time. Right now, though, I'd just like to give you a quick check, if that's all right.'

'OK.'

Beth checked Carla's pupils, BP and had a quick listen to her chest. 'Did you bang your head on impact?'

'It went back, then forward again.' Carla touched her neck and Beth tenderly palpated the area.

'Minor whiplash.' She wished she'd asked Charles for a cervical collar. 'What about the steering-wheel? Did you hit it as well?'

'I can't remember. I do feel sore around my ribs.'

'You'll have a seat-belt bruise but thank God you were wearing one. I can't hear anything out of the ordinary with your breathing but you may have cracked one or two ribs. Does it hurt to breathe?'

'A little. It's getting worse.'

Beth nodded. 'Unfortunately, that's quite normal but we'll keep an eye on you.' She stood from where she had been crouching. 'When the ambulance gets here, I'll be able to give you something for the pain. In the meantime, just try to stay as still as possible.'

Ryan came over with a policeman. Beth introduced everyone and the officer started interviewing Carla. Ryan put a hand on Beth's arm and gently eased her aside. 'How is she?'

'Shocked but not *in* shock…yet.'

'Admit her overnight?'

'I've already told her I want her in overnight. I'll write up the notes when the next ambulance gets here. What about us?'

'Do we have to stay in hospital overnight?' he teased, and she was so glad *Ryan* had stayed, rather than sending *Sir Ryan* to deal with things. 'If we did, tongues would surely wag.'

Beth laughed and playfully punched his arm. 'No. Do we have to give the police statements?'

'I've told them our side of the story but, yes, they'll want to talk with you at some point, although I'm hoping we can at least leave that until tomorrow. You look exhausted.'

'I am. I'm beat on my feet.'

'Beat?' Ryan smiled at her. 'There's that American slang again.'

She shrugged. 'It happens. You've got a bit of a British tinge to some of the words you say.'

'I do not,' he said indignantly.

'See. Right there. It's the way you enunciate your vowels. They're not as relaxed as an Aussie drawl.' She smiled up at him and felt her heart jump as he smiled back.

'You're getting punchy.' As though it were the most natural thing in the world, Ryan draped his arm protectively around her shoulders, urging her closer.

For a split second Beth forgot how to breathe, telling herself he was only trying to provide warmth to her cold body. The last thing he'd want was his new registrar getting hypothermia. Beth struggled to remember what he'd said last. Punchy. He'd said she was getting punchy.

'Punchy, eh? Now, there's a good Americanism. Spent some time in the States, did you?' She lifted one French-tipped nail and tapped his chest playfully.

Ryan breathed in deeply, shifting his body to accommodate hers more thoroughly. He was feeling a little punchy himself, or was he merely punch-drunk with his fascination of Beth?

'Hey. Cut it out.' He wriggled.

'Cut it out?' she asked, tapping his chest again. 'Yeah? And if I don't?'

His gaze widened and his smile grew. Didn't she know how adorable she was when she was like this? He was both bemused and delighted with her attitude. He grabbed her offending finger with his free hand to stop her from poking him—he was actually ticklish there. He slid his palm against hers, entwining their fingers.

The instant he laced their fingers together, she felt it. The instant, undeniable attraction that had been there between them since the first moment they'd laid eyes on each other.

'Then I won't be held responsible for my actions.' His voice was deep and thick, his quiet words washing over her, enveloping her in the world where only the two of them belonged.

The awareness between them was palpable and Beth's heart rate instantly increased, her lips parting to allow the pent-up air to escape. She sucked in a breath, her gaze never leaving his. She was mesmerised by him. Somehow he'd managed to break through several of her defences, walls she'd erected many years ago and which few men ever broke through or even attempted to. Not that Ryan was trampling on her emotions, quite the opposite. He was being so tender, so caring that she could feel herself growing more susceptible to him, lowering her resolve and letting her heart beat wildly with longing.

'Hmm,' she finally managed. 'That could be interesting.'

He raised one eyebrow at her reply. 'Are you…interested?' His voice was still intimate, the two of them back in their little bubble.

'In discovering the consequences or in discovering you?' Her voice was husky and she couldn't…or didn't want to hide it.

He allowed her a small smile for her effort to tease. 'A bit of both, I guess.'

Again they were having one conversation with words and another with their bodies. At some point he'd slipped his arm from her shoulder and slid it beneath the warmth of her coat, the heat of his firm, muscled arm pressing into her. The scent of him wound itself around her and, combined with her own pheromones, it was a heady combination.

'Beth, I've been trying to kiss you all night long but now that the moment is here, I'm not sure I'm able.'

She felt a wave of heat, then a wave of ice wash over her at his words. 'Is something wrong?'

He savoured the feel of her so close to him, his arm firm around her waist, his other hand holding her hand tight. 'We really shouldn't, you know,' he finally said.

'Get involved?'

'Yes, even though I want to.' Ryan slowly exhaled and leaned his forehead against hers. He closed his eyes, trying to work through a logical solution to this emotional problem…and therein lay his dilemma because when he was around Beth, logic seemed to disappear.

CHAPTER SIX

'EXCUSE me, Dr Durant?' The police officer hovered near them and it took a moment for Ryan to release her. Beth dragged in a breath and pulled herself together. No longer could she be the woman turning to mush in Ryan's arms. She had to be professional, in charge, under control.

'What can I help you with, Officer?' Beth was pleased at how normal her voice sounded, not all husky and desirous as it had been before.

'I just have a couple of questions.'

'I'll check on Carla,' Ryan offered, and as he walked away, Beth pulled her coat tightly around herself, feeling the loss of Ryan's body warmth. She answered the questions put to her and by the time she had finished, the ambulance had arrived for Carla.

'Will you be coming to the hospital?' Carla asked Beth as the stretcher was lifted into the ambulance.

'Unfortunately, no, but you'll be well looked after. Just let everyone take care of you, Carla.' Beth stepped back to allow Carla's friend, who had arrived to lend support, into the ambulance. She spoke to the paramedic before the doors were closed and with a sigh of relief she headed back to where Arnold and Ryan were waiting by the taxi.

'Are we free to go?' she asked Ryan.

'Yes, and Arnold here has offered to take us home, free of charge.'

Beth climbed into the back seat of the taxi and was surprised when Ryan went round to sit in the front passenger seat. Was he trying to put extra distance between them? He'd said he wasn't sure they should get involved and she knew he had a point, but right now she needed a little bit of comfort. With Natalie and Marty gone and her parents still overseas, she was beginning to feel quite lonely.

She pulled her coat more firmly around herself and buckled up. As the warmth of the taxi spread around her, she rested her head back and closed her eyes, wondering exactly what she should do about this deep-seated attraction she felt towards Ryan. Usually, with the guys she dated, she could tell within the first few hours where they were coming from, and if it didn't match up with where she was headed, she usually didn't bother seeing them again.

Natalie was the one who'd called it 'standard-dating'. Beth called it being picky. She needed to be picky. She needed to find a man she could settle down with who would not only accept her for who she was but accept her family as well. The last serious relationship she'd had had ended when Jeff had met her parents, and although he'd made other excuses as to why their relationship would never work, Beth knew the truth behind his fears.

All her life, her parents had told her she was special and they hadn't been talking about her brain or the things she would accomplish during her lifetime. Beth was a one-in-four miracle. A normal-sized child born to dwarf parents. Her parents had always been there, urging her to do her best in everything. They'd paid for her to attend medical school and they were a constant source of support—just like parents should be. As she'd grown up and had heard stories from her friends, Natalie included, about what their own parents had been like, Beth had realised that she wasn't special because she was normal-sized, she was special because she was loved by her parents.

Then there was the subject of children. There was a slim chance she might have a dwarfed child. The thought didn't bother her in the slightest, and while a lot depended on her husband's genetic make-up, she needed to find someone who felt the same way she did—that the child they conceived would be important to them regardless. Certainly, when Jeff had broken up with her, she'd raised those exact questions and although he'd denied it wouldn't make any difference, she'd seen the fear in his eyes. That's when the standard-dating and the check-list had come into play. She required a special man to appreciate her special circumstances.

Was Ryan that man?

She shook her head and sighed, pushing the thought from her mind. It was late, she was tired and she wasn't sure she could move her feet any more.

'Focus on the now,' she whispered.

'You all right, Beth?' Ryan asked as he glanced over his shoulder into the back seat.

'I'm fine,' she returned.

'We're almost there.' Ryan had been talking softly with Arnold, thinking that Beth had drifted off to sleep. He didn't want her to think he was being rude by not including her in their conversation, so he said, 'Arnold's of the opinion that everyone who drives on the roads should be trained in first aid.'

'Sounds like a good opinion,' Beth said. 'If only there was a way of getting governments to enforce it.'

They continued to talk on the issue until Arnold pulled up outside Marty's house. 'Here you are, folks, and as I said before, this ride is definitely on me.' He pulled out a business card and handed it to Ryan. 'And if either of you need transport, you give me a call. You were both marvellous tonight.'

'You were the marvellous one,' Beth said as she climbed from the car, her bag in hand. 'You kept everyone else—cars included—under control, not to mention providing us with a well-stocked medical kit.' Arnold had stepped from the driver's seat and quickly held the door for Beth. She leaned over and kissed his cheek. 'Thank *you*.'

'Oh, now, Dr Durant. You're gonna make me blush.' He handed her a card as well. 'I mean it. You call me if you need transport.'

'I most certainly will.'

Ryan shook Arnold's hand. 'Thanks for everything.'

'Glad to help.' Arnold climbed back into his taxi. 'You look after her now, you hear? She's one to hold on to, Dr Cooper.'

Beth felt slightly embarrassed at Arnold's words and glanced surreptitiously at Ryan to see how he'd taken them. Ryan merely smiled politely and waved as Arnold drove off. He turned to look at her, their eyes slowly adjusting to the darkness of the early morning. A streetlight two houses down shone minimal light on them and for a moment neither of them moved.

Beth wished he'd speak. Although she'd spent time with him, excited at the attraction they felt, the reality was she still didn't know much about him at all. Now she was going to be spending the night in the same house as him and possibly the next few weeks as well. She would work with him, she would live…no, not live, coexist…in the same house as him…yet she still knew very little about him.

Not that she thought he'd harm her in any way, she knew enough of him to be sure of that. Besides, Marty and Natalie wouldn't be trying to throw them together if they thought Ryan unsafe. No. Her thoughts were of the attraction that seemed to be growing stronger with each moment they spent together.

Now, as they stood in the dark, with the remnants of Arnold's words—that Ryan should hang on to her—floating in the air between them, Beth felt highly uncomfortable. She wished he'd say something but he simply stood there, looking down at her as though he were mesmerised.

Finally, he slowly exhaled and put his hand into his pocket, his gaze still locked on hers. The instant he moved towards the house, the sensor lights came on, blinding them both for a moment. Ryan reached for her free hand and led her up the path towards the front door. His hand was warm and made her own hand tingle. She would have to learn to control her reaction to him because if he touched her at work, even like this, she'd probably end up making a fool of herself.

'Nothing like coming back to reality with a thud,' he muttered.

'Pardon?' She was surprised at his words.

He dropped her hand, then opened the door and turned to look at her. 'Nothing. After you.' He waited for her to precede him into the house before he came in and shut the door behind them, locking it.

Beth stood in the entryway, not sure where to go next. 'I've never been here before,' she said softly.

'Oh. Sorry. I thought you had. In that case…' Ryan took a few steps to the opposite wall and flicked the light switch. 'Allow me to show you around.' He reached out to take her hand again but she stepped away.

'I'll just follow you.'

'Why don't you want to hold my hand, Beth?' he teased, trying to lighten the atmosphere around them. 'I don't bite.'

'That's not the point and you know perfectly well why I don't want to hold your hand.'

'I do?'

'Nothing like coming back to reality with a thud,' she repeated. 'We've come out of the bubble, Ryan. It was nice while it lasted but you're right. Reality is here now. We have to figure out whether we're both going to stay here, but first of all we have to survive a night in the same house.'

'Without me coming on too strong?' His grin was silly and enough to break the tension.

Beth glared at him for a moment, trying to hold onto her annoyance, but it didn't work. She smiled shyly and said, 'Stop teasing me, Ryan.'

'Why? You're so adorable when you're riled.'

'Stop it!' Beth demanded. Just when she thought the situation had been defused, he said things like that and made her want to grab him and kiss him. 'You don't tell a woman you find her adorable, sexy or anything else when you're trying to bring the tension down a notch in order for the two of you to get through the night alone.'

Ryan shoved both hands in his pockets and nodded. 'You're right, you're right. Let me give you a quick tour and then you can choose which bedroom you want and we can say goodnight.'

'Let me just sit down and take off my shoes,' she said, and he led her into the dining room and held out a chair.

'By all means. While you're doing that, I'll go turn on the heating.' He headed off, thinking the coolness of the house might actually help him concentrate on something other than Beth, as he doubted he'd be getting much sleep. She was right, though. They had to either put a stop to what was happening between them or else figure out the best way to handle it.

He'd been instantly attracted to women in the past but never to this extent. He put it down to something hereditary. His parents had felt that instant attraction and although they'd tried to deny it for a while, it had won out in the end and they were still happily married. Beth, however, was not his usual type of woman. He preferred brunettes and Beth was definitely blonde…a gorgeous, charming and funny blonde.

'Instant attraction,' he murmured, as he switched the heating on and turned the thermostat to high. He headed back to where he'd left her and stopped in the doorway to the dining room. Beth had not only taken off her coat and shoes but had taken her hair down as well, the pins and little flowers scattered on the table-top in front of her. She had her feet up on another chair, her eyes closed and her head back as she ran her fingers through her wavy blonde strands.

Her neck was long and gorgeous and his comment that he didn't bite made him realise he honestly wanted to nibble on her luscious neck…and work his way up to claim her most perfect lips with his. He watched her massaging her scalp for a few more moments before he turned away. He had to turn away. It was either that or walk over and help her to massage her scalp.

Ryan went through the house looking for Beth's bags and found them in one of the back bedrooms. He'd left his bags in the master bedroom at the front of the house when he'd come to pick Marty up for the wedding. He quickly took her things to the master bedroom, complete with *en suite*, knowing that would give her more privacy. He would be happier in the back bedroom, using the bathroom opposite it.

The heat was starting to come through now and he headed back to the kitchen, filled the kettle and switched it on. 'Tea?' he called. There was no way he could go back into that dining room and see her looking as mesmerising as she'd been before. They were alone now and both of them were tired and probably running on very little reserves. He knew from experience that when that happened, a person could say or do things they might definitely regret after a good night's sleep. He vowed that he wouldn't touch her…at least not tonight because even with his own reserves running low, he might not be able to resist just one kiss and the one thing he didn't want with Beth were regrets. They worked together, day in, day out, and as he was her boss, that threw another spanner into the works, especially as neither of them dated colleagues.

When he received no answer, he knew he had to go back in there. Steeling himself, he was met with the sight of Beth leaning forward, her head on the table, resting on her arm, her eyes closed. Her hair had fallen across her face and Ryan flexed his fingers, itching to touch the silky blonde strands.

He crossed to her and tenderly brushed the hair from her face, surprised to find it a little coarser than he'd thought. Then again, she'd had it curled and pinned and probably sprayed with all sorts of hair products to keep it in place for the wedding. He listened, realising her breathing was quite deep.

'Beth?' He called her name softly and gave her shoulder a gentle shake.

'Hmm?'

The soft murmured sound started cracking his resolve and he swallowed hard. 'Come on. Let's get you to bed.' With that, he broke the vow he'd made only seconds ago and scooped her gently into his arms. It was a place he liked having her and as this was the second time he'd held her like this, he realised it was something he could become quite accustomed to.

She sighed and snuggled close to him, making him almost falter in his step. The scent of peaches and wild flowers assailed his senses once again, just as it had every time she'd been close to him that night. It was a scent he could well get used to and he knew every time he did, it would drive him to distraction.

Unable to resist, he pressed a kiss to the top of her head in what he chided himself was a purely avuncular kiss, but he knew in reality it was the only way he'd let his lips touch her this evening. He breathed in deeply again, savouring the moment before he crossed to the bed.

'Beth? Can you stand?'

'Hmm?' came the reply again. Ryan slowly lowered her to the edge of the bed, and surprisingly, she was able to sit. Quickly, he flicked back the bedcovers, wondering whether she needed help getting out of her dress.

'No,' he growled, knowing there was no way he could handle such a sight tonight—not even if he pulled all his professionalism together. Right now she was more delectable than he'd found any other woman and if he wanted to remain a gentleman, he would need to leave her to fend for herself, even if it meant she slept in her dress.

He helped her to lie down, tucked her feet in and brushed the hair from her face once again. 'You're so beautiful, sweetheart,' he murmured, the backs of his fingers caressing her cheek. *Get out, get out,* said the voice inside his head, and after allowing himself another quick kiss to the top of her head, he almost sprinted from the room.

The kettle forgotten, Ryan switched off the lights as he walked through the house, adjusted the thermostat to a more reasonable level and headed for the bathroom. A cold shower was the only prescription likely to get him through the night.

In the morning, it took a while for Beth to realise where she was. After she'd opened her eyes she remained still, holding her breath as she tried to recall the events of the night before. She was in Nat and Marty's house and this must be their bedroom. She let out the breath she was holding and sat up, taking in her surroundings.

It was then she realised she was still in her bridesmaid's dress. Flicking back the covers, she swung her feet down and sat on the edge of the bed, realising Ryan must have carried her in. The last thing she remembered was taking off her shoes. As she couldn't see them, she realised they must still be in the dining room.

Her bags were at the end of the bed so she stood and unzipped her large suitcase, pulling out a change of clothes. 'Shower first.' Her stomach grumbled. 'Then food,' she promised. She pushed her hair from her eyes and muttered, 'Definitely shower.' She hated having so much gunk in her hair and couldn't wait to wash it all out.

Fifteen minutes later she was dressed in a tracksuit with a pair of runners on her cold feet, her damp hair hanging shiny and clean around her shoulders. Hesitantly, she headed to the kitchen and filled the coffee-maker. While that brewed, she collected her shoes, coat and a multitude of hairpins from the dining-room table and quickly returned them to her room.

Next was an inspection of the cupboards and refrigerator. Thankfully, as Marty had known someone would be staying here, he hadn't bothered to throw out any food that might go off, such as eggs, milk, butter and cheese. Beth licked her lips as she pulled things from the fridge.

Soon she had coffee brewed and eggs scrambling. She was just opening the overhead cupboards in search of the toaster when she heard a noise behind her. Spinning round, she hit her head on the cupboard door.

'Ow.'

'You all right?' Ryan asked as he walked into the kitchen. Beth turned to look at him, one hand rubbing her head. The hand stilled, her mouth hung open and her eyes drank him in. He was wearing a pair of well-worn black jeans and that was all! His torso was bare and Beth felt her mouth dry up completely as she took in his smooth skin, broad shoulders and the muscles that were defined as he ruffled his hands through his hair, tousling the dark locks even more.

'Eggs are about to burn,' he said, when she didn't answer his question. He moved around her and she quickly sidestepped him lest their bodies touched. Seeing his body was enough. Touching it would send her own senses into hyperdrive.

'Excuse me.' She forced her legs to move and headed directly for her bedroom, closing the door behind her and leaning against it for support. You can do this. You can do this. You're a doctor, for heaven's sake. You've seen men with their shirts off before and never had such a violent reaction. It's just a body. Albeit an amazing body but a body all the same. After a few more deep breaths she thought she might be able to head back to the kitchen but first she splashed some cold water on her face.

'Beth?' Ryan was calling. 'How many pieces of toast do you want?'

One more deep breath and then she opened her door and headed out. This time his body wasn't such a shock but it was still electrifying all her senses.

'How many pieces of toast would you like?'

'Uh…one. Thanks.' She followed his movements, her gaze caressing the smooth lines of his back. As he turned, she continued to feast her eyes on his washboard stomach that dipped teasingly beneath his jeans.

'Sure.' He put the toast down then pulled out some plates and cutlery. 'Take a seat,' he said, motioning to the bench stools. She did as she was asked, glad her legs didn't need to support her for a while.

'I guess you know your way around here pretty well.' Her voice was a little deeper than usual and she cleared her throat, hoping he'd put it down to early morning huskiness rather than desire caused by the sight of his naked torso.

'Sure. I've stayed here many times. Sleep well?'

'Out like a light.' Her gaze flicked up to meet his as he turned round and she wondered whether he'd just caught her ogling him. It was difficult not to look with such maleness spread before her. 'Do you cook? Marty's quite good at it.'

'Of course I do. Our mothers insisted we both learn all domestic duties from a young age. I started doing my own washing when I was ten. From the age of seven I was cooking a meal once a week.' He shrugged those broad, naked shoulders and Beth found herself sighing as she watched the action. She'd never been one to swoon at a guy but Ryan was leading her in directions she'd never thought she'd go. If only he'd go put a shirt on. 'When I was a teenager, I earned extra money by cleaning houses.'

It took her a moment to focus on his words and as he lifted the pan of eggs from the stove, she gasped in case he burnt himself. He was careful and did no such thing. 'Really? You cleaned houses?'

'Surprised?'

'A little.' Don't look at his chest. Don't look at his chest!

'Why? It was good practice for cleaning an operating theatre later in life.'

'That's usually left up to the theatre staff.'

'Not in the bush.'

'True. I keep forgetting you've worked elsewhere.' She forced her gaze down to the bench, her hands clenching at her sides. If she didn't get herself under control soon, she'd be retreating to her bedroom again. 'I guess cleaning houses and teenage boys don't usually go together. I thought you might have earned extra money playing the piano and that sort of thing. You're very good.'

'Thank you.' He took the toast out and buttered it before dishing out the eggs and putting her plate in front of her. 'I played in bars when I was older.'

She looked up to say thank you but the words stuck in her throat. Once more she was confronted with his body and the need to reach out and splay her hands over his chest was becoming almost impossible to fight.

'How do you take your coffee?'

Beth quickly raised her gaze and found his slightly amused. The rat. Did he know how badly he was affecting her? Was he doing it on purpose?

She swallowed uncomfortably. 'Just with milk.'

He poured a cup of black for himself and one for her before getting the milk out the fridge. 'I'm glad Marty left us with supplies, although we'll have to take stock of what we have and don't have. Want to go shopping after breakfast?'

'Sure. I guess.' Anything to get him to put a shirt on and get out of the house. She needed to be with people, crowds of people if she was going to be around Ryan for the rest of the day. Whatever it was between them, that strong emotional pull, it was starting to become too strong for her to resist...but resist she must.

She took a grateful sip of her coffee before realising this situation wasn't working. She simply could not stop herself from staring at his chest. 'You must be cold,' she found herself saying. 'Why don't you go put something on? Can't have the boss getting sick.'

'I'm fine.' He brushed her words away. 'I became well accustomed to the cold after spending time in London. This cold, especially with the heating on, is nothing.'

Beth had had enough. She slapped a palm down on the bench and glared at him. 'You don't understand, Ryan. Go put a shirt on.' She glared at him and he merely raised his eyebrows. A split second later, dawning realisation flickered in the blue depths.

'Ah. Sorry. Sure.' He headed off to his room and Beth covered her face with her hands. 'Sorry,' he reiterated as he came back, buttoning a casual, blue cotton shirt. 'I should have thought.' He pulled a kitchen stool around the bench and sat down opposite her.

Beth clenched her hands together and risked a glance at him. He looked incredible in the shirt, the sleeves still outlining the muscles beneath. It was better than before but the picture of his torso would be forever burned on her memory.

'No, I'm the one who's sorry, Ryan. You should have the right to dress however you like.'

'True, but as we're going to be living here together, I should have thought.' He'd been able to feel her visual caresses on him as he'd cooked breakfast and he'd certainly enjoyed them. He'd initially thought she'd just been staring at him to tease, to make him feel uncomfortable. He'd had no idea she felt as strongly as she did.

'About that...the...staying-here-together thing.' She took another sip of her coffee, hoping it would give her strength. She put her cup down and raised her eyes to his. 'I don't think it's going to work.'

'I promise to be appropriately clothed at all times.' He held up his fingers in the Scout salute.

'You were a Scout, too?'

'Absolutely, and I never break a Scout promise.' He started eating his breakfast and the tension that had been rampant between them dimmed slightly. 'Look, we can make this work. Both of us will be looking for alternative accommodation during the next three weeks. Add to that the fact I'll be gone for some of the time, so if we can just tough it out here, it will make life easier for both of us.'

'I know the logistics of the plan,' Beth said, looking down at the breakfast in front of her but not sure she could eat it now. 'I just hadn't planned on...on...' She reached for her coffee-cup again, unable to go on.

'On the mutual attraction we feel?'

Beth nodded.

'Neither did I.' Into his mind came the vision of her last night, stretched back on the chair, her neck long and luscious. No, he hadn't planned on it at all but it was there and it was up to the two of them to remain strong in whatever they decided and make things work out. 'It's probably just the romance of yesterday's wedding that is affecting us.'

'Yes.' Beth knew they were kidding themselves. Whatever it was between them, it had started from the first time they'd met six months ago. She'd been attracted to him but hadn't been impressed with his personality. Now, though, she was impressed with everything about him. Then again, for the past twenty-four hours she'd been given a glimpse of what Ryan was like *away* from a medical setting. 'You said last night you didn't think it was a good idea for us to get involved as we'll be working together, and I agree with you. I don't think we should. There's too much going on in my life at the moment and I'm sure you have more than enough to worry about, taking over the department and organising your teaching roster and...and everything.'

'Very true.'

'So the last thing either of us would have time for is working on a relationship.'

'Is that what you want?'

'A relationship?'

He nodded.

'Yes. Something wrong with that?'

'No. No. Not at all. It's good that you know what you want, what your goals are.' He concentrated on finishing his breakfast while Beth sipped her coffee, her desire for toast and eggs gone.

'But not for you?'

'I have no objection to other people having relationships.'

'Just not you.' Why did that thought depress her? Beth shook her head. 'How did we get onto this subject?'

'You wanted me to put a shirt on.'

'Look. It's no secret. I'm attracted to you but so is half the female population at the hospital.'

'Only half?' he asked with mock pain.

'Oh, the ego.' This time she laughed at the expression on his face. 'As I was saying, I'm attracted and we've acknowledged this but it can't go anywhere.'

'OK. Give me your reasons.'

'Well, we'll be working together for a start. What if we have an argument and it carries over into the job?'

'It wouldn't.'

'How can you be so sure? I watched Natalie and Marty avoid each other at work for a week.'

'One week? That's nothing. I moved to a war zone to avoid a girl.'

'See.'

'I was joking. Sort of.'

'Well, I'm not. Ryan, it's not going to work and we need to set down some ground rules right now.'

'Ground rules. Oh, yay. How I love 'em.'

'Ryan. Be serious.'

'I am being serious. My whole life since my knighthood has

consisted of one set of rules after another. I've grown used to them. So come on, Beth. Let's set down some ground rules. Rule number one—be appropriately dressed at all times. And that goes not just for me but you as well.'

She glanced down at her clothes. 'I'm appropriately dressed.'

'But you weren't yesterday.'

'I was in a bridesmaid's dress yesterday.'

'Exactly. So no more wearing things that cling to every curve of your body, and especially no off-the-shoulder clothes. It makes your neck way too inviting.'

If he'd wanted to throw her off balance, he'd succeeded. 'Oh.'

'Yes, "oh." I find you attractive as well so don't go thinking this is all one-sided and making me out to be the bad guy.'

'That wasn't my intention.'

'This is a two-way street. Open and honest communication is all we need to get through the next few weeks, which brings me to rule number two—no overnight guests. It's only for a few weeks and it's not fair to make the other person uncomfortable.'

'Agreed.'

'Your dating won't be affected so long as you don't bring any of them back here.'

'What? I don't sleep with them,' she retorted hotly, standing up from the stool to pace the floor. 'How dare you even imply that?'

'I'm sorry.' He came around the bench and crossed to her side.

'You don't know me at all, Ryan Cooper, and you have no idea at all what my reasons are for dating the way I do.'

'I know. I'm sorry.' He stopped her pacing by placing his hands on her shoulders and turning her to face him. 'I apologise.'

She was breathing hard, the action causing her chest to rise and fall, and Ryan was mesmerised for a moment before forcing his gaze to meet hers. His gut tightened, as it always did when he was this close to her. What was it about this woman that made him react this way? He watched as she clenched and unclenched her hands at her sides, trying to get herself under control. It was nice to know this thing between them wasn't all one-sided and seemed to stir her up as much as it did him.

One moment Beth was furious with him and the next she was fighting to keep her hands off him. The chest she'd been itching to touch was now so close to her, so near her hands… The temptation was causing her palms to perspire and after unclenching her hands one last time, she wiped them down her trackpants, the itching intensifying.

'You can let me go now.' Even as she whispered the words, she wished he wouldn't. She wished he'd gather her close and hold her as he'd held her last night. She wished he'd finally press his lips to hers so they could get it out of the way. It was a strange sensation to be feeling and she kept reminding herself she knew next to nothing about who Ryan Cooper really was. Usually, a man didn't get to kiss her until he'd at least passed a few rounds of her check-list requirements. She hadn't even begun to test Ryan yet the need to be held by him, to feel his warm mouth moving over hers, was starting to drive her insane. It wasn't logical…and she was always logical.

'Really?' His voice was equally as soft and intimate. 'Your body tells me another story. Do you really want me to let you go, Beth?'

She looked at his mouth while he spoke, finding it difficult to register the words he was saying. He was close, close enough for her to feel his warm breath on her face, and it was all she could do not to melt completely into his arms. Her tongue came out to wet her lips as she flicked her gaze up to his eyes, knowing the desire she saw there mirrored her own.

She swallowed. 'No.'

He gazed down into her eyes and slowly nodded. 'I didn't think so.'

Even his arrogance didn't bother her, which was strange because arrogance was something she didn't like and she had crossed many a man off her list because of it. This time, though, it wasn't conceited arrogance, it merely showed he knew the hold he had over her. She was justifying everything for him…and she didn't care. She wanted Ryan to kiss her and that was all there was to it.

'This is madness,' she said.

'True, but a madness we both want.'

'It's wrong.' She tried again to knock some sense into what was happening between them.

'Probably.'

'But I want you to kiss me so much.' As she said the words, she finally gave in to one thing she'd been dying to do. With her heart pounding wildly against her chest, she lifted her hands with agonising slowness, fingers splayed, and eventually brought them into contact with his chest. Her lips parted again to let the air escape as she touched him in such a glorious and intimate fashion. She swallowed nervously as the tingles from beneath her fingertips shot up her arm and exploded throughout her entire body.

He dragged in a breath and exhaled harshly at the touch. Feeling her hands on his body, feeling the desire that was running through both of them, feeling a way he'd never felt before, made the experience of such a simple touch more intense, more satisfying than anything he'd felt in years.

He put his head back and closed his eyes, his own hands gripping her shoulders more firmly as she continued to wreak havoc with his senses. When her fingers trailed downwards and slipped beneath his shirt, her fingernails slightly grazing his abdomen, his muscles instinctively tightened and a low moan escaped from his lips.

Now her fingers traced the pattern they'd explored before but this time there was only skin to skin, no pesky fabric to bother them. With a slight step closer she edged her fingers around to his back, their trails blazing fire right through him.

'Beth.' Her name felt perfect coming from his lips and she loved the way it sounded. Deep, guttural, yet needy. She closed her eyes, almost hyperventilating at the liberties he was letting her take. The feel of his warm, smooth skin was intoxicating and enough to turn her mind to mush. Nothing else in the world existed. It was just the two of them. No problems, no hospital, no living issues…no nothing.

His hands on her shoulders gripped tighter still and she loved that she could affect him so much. He edged her closer, his hands sliding down her back until her chest was pressed against his. She lifted her head at the same time he lowered his.

Both of them opened their eyes to look at each other, to make sure that before whatever this was that existed between them burned totally out of control they were both still on the same wavelength. When they were poised on the brink of finally giving in, Ryan hesitated for a moment.

Beth felt it and decided she was going to call him on it. 'What's wrong?'

He gazed down into her face and shook his head. 'Nothing.'

'You do want this, don't you?' The words were breathless and hard to utter but she didn't want him to have regrets. She knew she certainly didn't.

'Usually when I get this close to you, we get interrupted.'

'You *want* to get interrupted?'

'No.' He shifted against her and her breath caught in her throat as another wave of out-of-control sensation swept through her body. 'No,' he said more fiercely. 'I want to kiss you, Beth. I've wanted that for so very long.'

'Then stop yammering and put your mouth where it ought to be,' she insisted impatiently.

'On yours?' He raised one eyebrow, enjoying the further heightening of the sensations coursing between them and through them. Teasing Beth was as exciting as holding her in his arms, but she had a point. 'Ready?'

She nodded once, growing more nervous and excited with each passing moment. This was it. He was *finally* going to kiss her.

CHAPTER SEVEN

WHEN his mouth came into contact with hers, they melted into each other.

She'd expected it to start off tentative and then heat up instantly, but once more she was surprised by the tenderness and gentleness of the man in her arms. It was as though he'd waited far too long to be where he now was to rush things. Instead, he wanted to savour.

That first contact was electrifying and as though she were caught up in a cloud-filled dream; his lips savoured the taste of her, giving their other senses time to mingle. In slow motion, the tip of his tongue gently touched her lips and she found herself turning into a boneless mass, her insides liquefied into total submission.

She parted her lips, eager to give him what he was searching for, but again he took his time, pressing small kisses to her lips with just a hint of tongue. She breathed in sharply, unable to control the slight quivering of her body. His scent was stronger now and more addictive than before, and as she breathed out, she trailed her fingers up and down his back.

She felt the vibrations of the long, drawn-out moan that finally escaped him as he gathered her as close as he possibly could, both of them eager for as much contact as they could get. He still didn't deepen the kiss, wanting to take his time to explore every curve, every nuance of her delicious mouth. The desire burning within him was definitely becoming harder to control, but control it he would. Her mouth was more delicious than he could possibly have imagined and the way she willingly responded to him was almost enough to make him break his resolve and give in to the hungry cravings he could feel gnawing deeply at both of them.

The ringing in his ears began softly and he murmured his satisfaction when she traced the outline of his lips with her tongue. The hunger grew another notch. When she trailed her fingers up his back and then gently scratched her nails down, making him arch his back, the hunger grew again.

The ringing became louder, and belatedly he realised it was the phone. Dredging superhuman effort from somewhere, he eased back.

'Leave it,' she whispered, pressing kisses to his jaw.

'I can't.' Already he was trying to disengage himself from her hold. 'It might be the hospital.'

'Let the machine get it.'

'I can't,' he said again, and put her from him. In two short strides he was across the room, dragging in a much-needed breath and raking his hand through his hair. 'Dr Cooper,' he said after lifting the receiver, his voice still thick with desire.

Beth couldn't move. She was stunned he'd left her…left her wanting more and more of those deliciously seductive kisses. She watched and listened to him.

'No. You didn't wake me. What's the problem?' He didn't look at her. Instead, he pulled the notepad and pen that sat by the phone into his hands and began writing.

She watched him for a second longer, amazed he seemed totally in control of all his faculties while her body was still waiting for her brain to come back on line. It was then Beth realised the moment was well and truly over and she looked a right fool standing where he'd left her, hands hanging limply at her sides. Frustration and anger, mixed with embarrassment and a touch of self-consciousness, burned within her and she realised she'd better move before he ended his call.

Not saying a word, she stalked to her room and picked up the house keys Natalie had given her. She hunted through her bag for her MP3 player, hung it around her neck and headed out the door, fitting the earplugs into place as she went.

After a kiss like that, cut short without a proper resolution, she was left to work off her frustrations another way. She slipped out, closing the door behind her, and ran down the path, turning left at the end. She wasn't too familiar with this part of town but none of that mattered as the music set her pace.

As her feet pounded the pavement, she tried to figure out how Ryan could turn his emotions on and off like a tap. One moment he was kissing her in the most tantalising way and the next he was calmly answering the phone, taking notes. It was a good five minutes since he'd ended the kiss and her body was still trembling.

Then there were other questions that came to mind such as, what now? They'd kissed. They were colleagues. She wanted a relationship, he didn't. So…what now?

'You shouldn't have kissed him,' she mumbled as she turned the corner and followed a sign pointing to the jogging track, but even as the words tumbled out her mouth she knew it was point-less to think of it that way. She would have kissed him sooner or later and perhaps it was just as well it had been sooner. Now, hopefully, they could gain some perspective regarding their mu-tual attraction. Friends and colleagues? More than friends? What about her check-list? She'd better make a start if she planned on dating Ryan.

Although, when she thought about it, she realised she already had a few answers, especially to the 'chemistry' and 'family' questions. The chemistry between them was so palpable it was little wonder they hadn't set that room on fire with that kiss. She loved the teasing banter beforehand, never having felt comfort-able with it, but Ryan did it with such flair, such ease it had only added to the romance of the moment.

Regarding her 'family' questions, she'd met his parents yes-terday at the wedding and it was clear that they were very close to their son. His friendship with Marty was also testament to his ability to have long-term relationships and to care about people.

All these things were on her check-list because family was vitally important to her. Her parents were the most amazing people she knew, and although she'd endured ridicule and scorn through high school and even medical school, simply because her parents were different, she wouldn't have them any other way.

Now, though, her motive for screening the man she would eventually marry so closely was to not only protect herself but her parents as well from unnecessary ridicule. If the man she fell in love with couldn't accept her parents, then he was not the man for her.

Reaching the jogging track, she realised she felt less frustrated about Ryan and more interested to see how he passed the rest of the tests she would give him. Secretly, a part of her hoped he would because she definitely wanted more of those electrifying kisses.

Glad it wasn't raining and that her body had now warmed up, she began to sprint around the track, concentrating on her stride and breathing. When she arrived back at the house about an hour later, there was no sign of him. 'Ryan?' she called as she walked around. Tentatively, she headed down to the rear of the house. 'Ryan?' There was no sign of him. It was then she thought to check the garage and when she did, she found Marty's four-wheel-drive gone.

He'd been on the phone when she'd left and it had sounded as though it had been the hospital so the chances were that's where he'd gone. She went into the kitchen, hungry from her run and also from the fact that she'd passed on breakfast.

The morning dishes had been cleared and stacked in the dishwasher and she felt a pang of guilt at having left him to clean everything up. Perhaps she should make dinner tonight to make it up to him.

'No, Beth,' she cautioned herself. 'You are sharing a house, not living together.' She yanked open the fridge, pulled out some bread and peanut butter and poured herself a glass of water. Besides, he might not even be back by dinnertime, preferring to stay at the hospital rather than being alone with her.

She didn't begrudge him going to the hospital—after all, she completely understood what was involved. It was just the way he'd dropped her like a hot potato as soon as the phone had rung. No woman, especially one in the throes of her first kiss with a man she'd been fantasising about since Christmas, liked to be dropped that quickly.

She sat down to eat her sandwich and then saw a note next to the telephone. He'd left her a note. She smiled shyly to herself. Was it just a few lines to say he was sorry their kiss had been interrupted and that he'd be more than willing to pick up where they'd left off when he returned?

Beth read the note—her attitude changing as the words sunk in. No confessions of undying love or even that he'd enjoyed the kiss. No. This note had been written by a totally annoyed man, angry that she'd left without a word and that she'd gone without her cellphone. True, she usually took it with her when she jogged but she'd been so desperate to get out of the house that she'd forgotten. Besides, she wasn't on call.

Ryan had written that he'd gone to the hospital and wasn't sure when he'd be back. He hadn't signed the note but even the firmness of the pen on the paper indicated he'd been annoyed when he'd written it.

Beth scrunched up the note and tossed it over her shoulder. How dared he? She wasn't his girlfriend, she wasn't his wife and here, at Nat and Marty's, she wasn't even his registrar. She didn't have to tell him where she was going. True, she should have taken her phone, but sometimes people forgot things and in this instance, she'd forgotten. No big deal.

She finished her sandwich, stacked her dishes and wiped the bench, picking up his note and filing it in the appropriate place—the bin. She called the hospital to check on their mystery patient from last night and also to see how Carla was doing.

Tristan was in the ward and she spoke to him.

'Ms Mystery still hasn't been identified but after many painstaking hours in Theatre by yours truly, she spent the night in High Dependency and her situation hasn't changed.'

'Do you know why she was wandering about in the middle of the road?'

'High as a kite. The tests we did before taking her to Theatre confirmed a high level of ecstasy in her bloodstream.'

'And Carla?'

'She's OK. The police have been to talk to her again but I think she'll be right as rain this morning, although I have prescribed counselling.'

'Good.'

'How about you? How did the wedding go? Did you save me a piece of cake?'

'No. Was I supposed to?'

'Beth, Beth, Beth,' he muttered, then laughed. 'I guess I'll get over it one day.'

'You can eat cake at my wedding.'

'Oh, really? And when's that?'

She snorted. 'Your guess is as good as mine.'

'So how did things go with you and Sir Ryan yesterday? No fights? You both behaved yourselves?'

Beth was so glad she wasn't having this inquisition face to face because she was already blushing and Tristan had a way of pulling details from her she usually wouldn't have shared. 'Of course. Natalie was beautiful, Marty was mesmerised and the attendants behaved themselves. It was a fairy-tale.'

'Hmm. Why don't I completely believe you? Not the part about the fairy-tale, though. I'm sure it was perfect for Natalie.'

'Look. I've gotta call and check in with the police to see what's happening with last night's accident so I'll see you tomorrow.'

'Just a moment,' Tristan said, and she could hear him talking to someone. He came back a moment later. 'I've gotta go, Beth. Sir Ryan's come in to see a patient.'

'Yeah, I know.' The words were out of her mouth before she could stop them.

'How do you know?'

'Um…'

'Never mind. I'll get the info out of you later. This isn't over.'

He disconnected the call. Beth closed her eyes and groaned. When Tristan found out she and Ryan were living in the same house, he'd go to town on her, teasing and cajoling and probably helping the matchmaking process along, just like everyone else seemed happy enough to do.

Beth shook her head and decided she needed to focus on something else. Something not Ryan! She dialled the number of the police station and was able to give the information they required over the phone.

'We'll get everything typed up and sent to the hospital for your signature,' the officer said.

She sighed with relief when she eventually hung up, glad everything was now sorted. What to do now? She wasn't used to being at a loose end and thoughts of Ryan and the electrifying kiss filled her mind. She paced around the house a few times before deciding her excess energy would be better spent doing something productive. Pushing all thoughts of Ryan from her head, she pulled the pad and pen from by the phone and started making a shopping list.

She wouldn't get much as she didn't have a car to carry it in, Natalie having loaned her car to her brother who was going on a driving holiday. Once her list was done, she put her phone and house keys in her bag and wrote a note to Ryan—in case he returned in her absence—telling him she was at the grocery store and giving him her cellphone number before heading out.

The entire time she walked to the shops and toiled around the shelves she was trying not to fume at the man's audacity. Who'd elected him head of the household? Just because he was in charge at the hospital, that didn't mean she was going to let him dictate rules and regulations at the house. As she came out of the store, she passed a real estate agency and picked up their latest listings. She was determined to find somewhere else to live, and fast.

Beth walked home, trying to beat the threatening clouds, and was just at the gate outside the house when her cellphone started ringing. She rushed to the verandah and put the groceries down, hunting through her bag for the phone and house keys at the same time.

She found the keys first and fitted one into the lock as her other hand found the phone. She connected the call. 'Dr Durant.' The line went dead. Growling, she tossed it back into her bag, continued opening the door and picked up the groceries.

'There you are.' Ryan startled her by appearing suddenly. 'I was just trying to call you.'

She didn't say a word and she doubted he would have even known she was annoyed except for the small growl that came from deep in her throat.

'Let me help you with those.' He took the bags from her and carried them through to the kitchen. He was dressed in trousers and a casual sweater—definitely the wardrobe of Sir Ryan, rather than the half-naked man she'd been faced with that morning. A picture of his body flashed through her mind before she shoved it aside. He might be handsome and gorgeous and kiss like an absolute dream, but he was also dictatorial and arrogant—two qualities she *wasn't* looking for in a man.

She closed the front door and headed into the kitchen, where he was already sorting through the bags and putting things away. 'We've got to be quick.'

'Why? Have you got to rush back to the hospital?'

'No.' He seemed surprised at her attitude. 'I've just received a call from the airport.'

'Sydney airport?'

'Yes.' He stopped what he was doing and crossed to her side, tenderly taking her hands in his. It looked as though 'Ryan' had come back and 'Sir Ryan' had been left at the hospital. 'Beth, your parents are on a flight due to land in Sydney in two hours' time. Your father's not well.'

She felt the blood drain from her body and her knees go weak. Panic gripped her as she stared at him, her mind frantically trying to take in what he was saying. 'Is…is he stable? Did they say what was wrong with him?'

'They couldn't give me the details as I'm not next of kin. They needed to notify you, for legal purposes but also in case you wanted to be there when your parents landed.'

'They weren't due back for another few weeks.'

'Looks as though they changed their plans.'

Beth dropped his hands and turned away. 'Why didn't Dad call me before they left?' she whispered, her mind trying to work through things.

'Is your dad sick in some way?'

'He has spinal problems.' Beth looked at Ryan, deciding she may as well get this part of her check-list over and done with right now. 'My parents are dwarfs.'

Ryan didn't bat an eyelid at this information. He didn't baulk, he didn't frown. He merely nodded, indicating she should continue.

Thrown for a moment by his lack of reaction, she cleared her throat. 'He…er…he's been having treatment for years but when I saw him a few weeks ago when we caught up in the States, he was fine. They were going to do some more touring in America before coming home. I should have insisted they come back with me.' She thought back. 'But he was fine then.'

'There's no point in second-guessing what you should have done. The point is they're on their way back now and we need to get you to the airport. Do you want to change?'

She glanced down at her clothes. 'Yes.' His words sank in. 'Yes,' she said, more vehemently.

'All right. Go get changed, I'll put the groceries away. We'll take Marty's car.'

'No. We might need—' She stopped, her mind clearing as she turned and headed for the phone. 'Just let me call and speak to someone to find out what exactly the problem is. Chances are he'll need to be taken directly to hospital.'

'Who does he usually see?'

'Phil Brooker. He's head of the spinal unit at St Gregory's. I'll call him once I've spoken to the airline.'

While she had been speaking, Ryan had continued putting away the shopping. He put the real estate guide on the bench. 'Oh, good. I was going to pick one up,' he murmured.

Beth dialled the number Ryan had written down for the airline and waited to be connected. She spoke to someone who said they'd connect her to someone else. She paced back and forth while she waited.

'On hold?'

'Yes.'

He held his hand out for the receiver. 'Go get changed. I'll call you when they come on the line.'

'No, it's—'

'Beth, stop arguing with me.' He snatched the receiver from her and gave her a gentle shove in the direction of her room. 'The sooner you're dressed, the sooner we can go.'

'We'll call Arnold,' she said, snapping her fingers. 'Where is that card of his?'

'I can take you.'

'And if we need to return in the ambulance?'

It was his turn to pause. 'Good thinking.' He pulled his cellphone from his pocket. 'I'll call Arnold while I'm waiting for the airline to get their act together.'

'I can call Arnold. Where did I put his card?' She frowned and looked around her.

'Beth! Get changed. I'll take care of the calls. Believe it or not, I know how to multi-task…to a certain extent,' he added with a sheepish smile. 'Now go.'

'All right, all right!' She stormed off to her bedroom, knowing he was right and momentarily disliking him for it. Half an hour later she was changed, they were in the taxi and were heading to the airport.

'What did the airline say about your father?' Ryan asked softly as he took her hand in his. She'd been pleased when he'd opted to sit in the back with her because right now, even though her mind was whirling with the possible treatments her dad might need, she also needed support and comfort. It seemed Ryan instinctively realised this because he was certainly providing it.

'She said he was complaining of severe back pain and that his medication didn't seem to be working. I asked a few questions and she relayed them to him. His fingers are numb and he's had difficulty walking for the last few days, which is why they decided to come home early. He saw a colleague of mine before he left and was cleared to fly.'

'Loss of bladder control?'

'Yes.' Beth looked down at their entwined hands. 'I wish I'd stayed and flown back with them.'

'You had a wedding to go to, they had other plans, he was checked by a doctor before flying. All bases were covered, Beth. Sometimes things just happen.'

She glanced up at him and smiled slightly. 'I know.' She paused, realising how much strength she was drawing from him. 'Thanks for coming with me, Ryan.'

'I wasn't busy.'

'Yes, you were. You were probably going to head back to the hospital and put in some more time.'

He shrugged. 'Just paperwork. It'll wait.'

'Really? I thought you'd gone to see a patient.'

He gave her an odd look. 'You've spoken to Tristan?'

'Yes.'

'Have you also contacted the police?'

'All done.'

'Good.'

They were silent for a moment, then Beth asked, 'Do you enjoy the paperwork?'

'Find me a person who does! No. Not particularly. I'm a doctor first and foremost, but I think I've adjusted well enough to my new responsibilities.'

'Because you had to?'

He thought about that for a moment, wondering how to tell her of the constricting bonds he'd felt ever since being knighted. Eventually, he shrugged. 'I guess you could say that.'

'Are you happy, though?'

'Sure. I love helping people, making them better. I like teaching other doctors my new technique to make life easier for everyone.'

Beth nodded. 'That's very noble of you.'

He chuckled. 'Hardly.' They were silent for a moment before he asked softly. 'How are you holding up?'

'I'm trying not to over-think the situation.'

'Do you think your father will need an operation?'

'I do.' She glanced down again, feeling the tears prick behind her eyes. Desperate to hold herself together, she dragged in a breath and forced herself to smile. 'But I guess we'll see what Phil says first.'

'What did he say when you spoke to him?'

'Phil suggested we send the ambulance and for me to monitor and provide necessary pain relief. He'd get the MRI organised.'

'If he needs surgery, do you think Phil will do a CT myelogram?'

'He's done one before but I think the MRI first will be the best bet.'

'Your father's had spinal surgery before?'

'Several times.'

'We're almost there,' Arnold announced. 'You want me to wait while you go in, Dr Cooper?'

'Yes, please, Arnold.'

'Right you are, then.'

'You go and see what's happening with the flight, Beth. I'll locate the ambulance.'

'OK.'

He gave her hand one last squeeze before they climbed from the taxi. Beth rushed into the airport and went directly to the arrivals counter. 'My name is Beth Durant and my parents are on a flight coming in from the States. My father's ill.'

The man behind the desk nodded as she spoke. 'We've been expecting you, Dr Durant. The aircraft is on the runway and that's where the ambulance was sent.' He pulled out a map and highlighted the roads they needed to take to get into the restricted area. 'I have a pass here for you and the necessary papers you'll need to show at the checkpoints.'

'Thank you. Thank you so much.' She gathered up the papers and headed back out to the taxi. Arnold was waiting patiently for her. 'Where's Ryan?'

'He hasn't come back yet.'

Beth handed the map to Arnold. 'This is where we need to go.'

Arnold studied the map. 'I know how to get there. You got the papers we need?' Again, she handed them over.

'Good. Look, here's Dr Cooper now.'

'Get in,' Beth called, and Ryan climbed in.

The instant his door was closed, Arnold took off. Beth explained what was happening.

'You'll still need to be scanned before entering the secure area,' Ryan told her.

'I don't care so long as I can get to my dad.'

Ryan took her hand again. 'He'll be fine.'

By the time they found the right gate, Beth's nerves were at breaking point. The medical scenarios she'd been concentrating on during the long ride to the airport left her and now all she was was total concern for her father. He was getting fragile, older and breakable and it scared her.

'He'll be OK,' Ryan reiterated.

'I hope so.' Beth shook her head, her eyes filling with tears again.

'Hey. You need to stop that now and be strong for him and your mother. Cry later, Beth, but for now pull it together.'

Ryan's words penetrated the fuzz around her brain. 'You're right.'

'Of course I am.'

Arnold brought the car up to the checkpoint and showed the papers. He was then told to park the taxi and for all of them to get out of the vehicle.

'Dr Durant?' The security guard checked her pass. 'This way.'

'What about him?' She pointed to Ryan. 'He's my colleague.'

'Do you have a pass for him?'

'They didn't give me one.'

'Then he doesn't go in.'

Beth glanced over her shoulder at Ryan.

'I'll get a pass and meet you in there,' Ryan promised. 'Go.'

Beth nodded, not sure she could speak. She felt so lonely being taken through the checkpoints and when she buzzed twice going through the scanners, she felt as though her nerves were going to completely snap.

'Take off your shoes, ma'am,' the security guard suggested, and Beth quickly slipped off her shoes and went through, thankfully not buzzing this time. She collected her belongings and after taking some deep breaths, she headed out to where the ambulance waited on the apron.

'Beth.' It was Charles and she breathed a sigh of relief as she headed over to him.

'Thank goodness it's you and not someone I don't know.'

'What are you doing here?'

She pointed to the plane, which was taxiing into position near them. 'My dad's on the plane. He's the one who needs the ambulance.'

Charles sighed. 'I'm sorry, Beth.'

'I just need to see how bad he is.' She watched as the plane came to a stop.

'The information I received as we came through was that the patient was stable. We'll be going in through the rear doors.'

Beth nodded at this explanation. 'I suppose you've done this type of thing before?'

'Sure have.'

The person in charge of the ground crew motioned for them to come over. Charles and his colleague took the stretcher and equipment out of the waiting ambulance and headed towards the portable lift, which would raise them up to the rear door. Beth glanced over her shoulder, hoping against hope to see Ryan heading towards her.

He was!

CHAPTER EIGHT

SHE knew she was relying on him too much, but right at that moment, she needed the support of someone strong and Ryan had already proved himself to be both supportive *and* strong in the face of adversity. Another thing she could cross off her check-list.

'Come on.' He came up beside her, grabbing her hand and pulling her along, not losing pace in his stride. 'Are you happy for me to take the lead on this?'

'Well…I know dad's condition better than you.'

'What's his name?'

'Daniel. I'll be fine once I see him.'

'I just don't want you to be under any extra pressure.'

'I know, but a lot of doctors are clueless about how best to treat my dad.'

Any other questions Ryan might have asked were cut short as the stretcher was put on the portable lift. Ryan and Beth stepped on beside it and soon they were being lifted up. When they reached the open rear doors of the plane, the lift was connected in place. Beth rushed forward into the plane, not waiting for anyone else.

Her mother sat next to her father, calmly holding his hand and talking with the flight attendant. The instant she saw Beth she held out her hand and Beth went willingly. She crouched down and the two quickly embraced. Then she turned to the man lying back on the reclined seat. She kissed his forehead and smiled down at him, whispering something that brought a tiny smile to the older man's face.

'I know you've taken your prescribed medicine. Is that all or have you had something else?'

'That's all,' Daniel Durant replied, his voice soft but laced with pain. 'It's bad, baby.'

'I know, Dad. Phil's waiting for you at the hospital. Let me give you something for the pain so we can move you.'

Ryan walked over and smiled down at her father. 'Hi, I'm Ryan. I'm a colleague of Beth's.' He looked down at Daniel. 'Are you allergic to anything, Mr Durant?'

'Morphine works well,' Beth answered. 'I'll get it.'

She crossed to where Charles was getting things ready to transfer her father out of the plane. 'Morphine, please.' She told him the dosage. 'Get a cervical collar on him and once the morphine's done its job, we'll get him moved.' She rattled off the list of medications her father took and Charles wrote them down before getting the morphine organised.

When she turned back she found Ryan crouched by her father, stethoscope in his ears, doing the neurovascular observations. 'Help Ryan,' she told Charles, and he headed over to measure Daniel's oxygen levels as well as pulse and BP. She handed the injection of morphine over to Ryan to administer.

They made sure Daniel was stabilised and that the morphine had started working before they attempted moving him. Beth left the lifting to Ryan and Charles, and as soon as her father was on the ambulance stretcher and secured, she let out a sigh of relief.

Her mother was busy thanking the flight attendants for their support and help. Beth added her thanks as well before taking her mother's hand. 'Let's get into the lift first so we're not in the way when they bring the stretcher out.'

'Good idea.' They took the careful step onto the lift and walked to the back corner. Isabelle looked up at her daughter. 'So, Ryan…is that his name?'

'Yes. He's Marty's cousin.'

'Of course. I remember now. He's the one you told us about—the one you had a special dinner for last Christmas.'

'I wasn't the only one there, Mum. It was a business dinner.'

'Of course, dear. I didn't mean to imply otherwise.' Isabelle paused. 'He's very handsome.'

Beth shrugged.

'You can't fool your own mother, Beth.'

'I can try,' she said dryly, and Isabelle laughed. She was such a beautiful woman, with the same blonde hair and brown eyes as Beth, and her laugh had always managed to bring a smile to everyone's face and this time was no exception.

'Fool me by all means, dear, but just don't go fooling yourself.' Isabelle took Beth's hand in hers, her eyes growing solemn for a moment. 'Your dad'll be fine.'

'I know.' They were starting to bring the stretcher out now.

'He needs another operation, doesn't he,' Isabelle stated rhetorically.

'It wouldn't surprise me, but let's get him to the hospital so Phil can look at him and do some tests.'

Isabelle sighed and shifted over to make more room for everyone.

'How are you holding up, Mrs Durant?' Ryan asked once they were all in and the lift started its descent.

'Oh, I'm just fine, Ryan. May I call you Ryan?'

He seemed taken aback for the moment. 'Of course.'

'Daniel just loves the attention, don't you, dear?'

Daniel mumbled something but it was incoherent. 'See?' Isabelle continued with a lilting laugh. 'Even with medication and that collar thing around his neck, he still wants to talk and get the attention.'

Beth smiled at her mother, knowing this was the way her mother coped with these types of situations. 'You can't resist teasing him, can you?'

'He wouldn't have it any other way, would you, dear?' Again Daniel tried to mumble something. 'See?' Isabelle smiled at the people around them and everyone seemed to relax a little. 'I was thinking, dear.' She turned to face Beth. 'I need somewhere to stay tonight. With our house still being rented and all, I've got nowhere to sleep.'

'Don't worry, Mum. You can stay in the hospital's residential wing.'

'Oh. I thought that was only for doctors and nurses.'

'No. Families as well. I'll get it organised once we arrive at the hospital. That way, you'll be nice and close to Dad.'

'Arnold's still waiting,' Ryan pointed out.

'Yes. Good thinking. Arnold, he's the taxi driver who brought us here. He can take you to the hospital while Ryan and I travel in the ambulance.'

'You know a taxi driver?' Isabelle asked.

'Long story.' Beth glanced at Ryan and both of them smiled.

'I look forward to hearing it,' Isabelle said, taking in the shared glance. The lift lurched a little as it came to the end of its descent and Beth walked her mother through the checkpoint and out to where Arnold was indeed still waiting with his taxi.

Beth introduced them and Arnold greeted Isabelle warmly. 'I'd be happy to take you wherever you need to go. Dr Durant and Dr Cooper are absolutely wonderful and I'm so happy to be able to help them out so soon after we met.'

Isabelle continued to be intrigued and Beth laughed. 'Arnold can tell you the whole story on the way to the hospital.'

'I am *definitely* looking forward to it, especially if it has something to do with the delicious Dr Cooper. He's just gorgeous, Beth.' Her mother looked sternly at her. 'I hope you're going to keep him around for quite a while, not your usual five minutes.'

Arnold seemed surprised. 'You mean you're not together?'

Beth was totally embarrassed. 'Er…no.'

'Huh!' Arnold frowned.

'Never mind,' Isabelle said, but Beth could tell from the grin on her mother's face that this was not going to be the end of the interrogation regarding Ryan. She helped her mother into the car before leaning down to kiss her cheek.

'Due to the flashing lights and sirens on the ambulance, we'll get to the hospital before you so have me paged when you arrive.'

'I will, dear.' Isabelle squeezed her daughter's hand and a shimmer of tears came into her eyes. 'He'll be all right. I just know it.'

Beth smiled reassuringly, hoping her mother was right. 'See you later.' She shut the door and watched for a moment as Arnold drove away before she turned and headed back to the checkpoint. This time she took her shoes off before going through the detectors and thankfully no alarms beeped.

Ryan was walking towards her and pointed at her feet. 'They check for foot odour, too?'

She slipped her shoes back on. 'Very funny.' She started walking towards the ambulance. 'How is he?'

'Holding his own for the moment. How about you?'

'I'm better now that I've seen him.'

'And your mum?'

Beth shrugged. 'She's just Mum. She's always calm when he's sick and then later, when he starts getting better, she usually falls apart.' She was still waiting for him to comment on her parents' size, to ask her questions, but it didn't come. Instead, he began talking about the severity of her father's myelopathy.

'The spinal cord dysfunction is quite severe.'

'I know. He's had quite a number of operations over the years and Phil's told him he may end up in a wheelchair. Phil's been treating Dad for years, long before I started studying medicine.' They reached the ambulance and Beth climbed inside to check her father once more. 'You still behaving yourself, Dad?'

'Yes,' came his mumbled reply. 'Is this thing really necessary?' He glanced down at the cervical collar around his neck.

'Yes, it is.'

'Bossy-boots,' he grumbled, and closed his eyes.

'All set to go?' Charles asked as he came to close the back doors after Ryan had climbed in beside Beth.

'Ready,' he replied, and Charles obligingly shut the door. Soon they were on their way and at the checkpoint they handed back their passes and signed several documents before they could leave that section of the airport.

Beth and Ryan set about doing her father's observations. 'How's the numbness in your fingers, Dad?'

'Still there. Very annoying.'

'I can imagine.'

'Daniel, can you feel the muscles in your legs and arms contracting and relaxing?' Ryan asked as he watched Daniel's legs repetitively go through the action.

'Sort of.'

'It's clonus,' Beth stated softly. 'A common reaction to myelopathy. So is hyperreflexia. The patient has no control over the contractions.'

'So this has happened before?'

'Yes.'

Ryan merely nodded. They continued with the observations. By the time they arrived at the hospital Beth was feeling much better about her father's prognosis. As they walked into A and E, she was greeted warmly by several of the staff, all of them vowing to do whatever it took to look after her father. Although there was gossip and rumour and a lot of other things that went on with the daily grind of hospital life, one thing she loved about St Gregory's was that they looked after their own. Ryan had become a little more aloof as they'd neared the hospital and she realised he was slipping back into Sir Ryan mode.

Phil greeted her warmly, kissing her cheek like the old family friend he'd become, before turning his attention to Daniel. 'What have you been doing with yourself?' he quizzed his supine patient. 'Scaring your wife and daughter, eh? Well, we'll sort you out.'

Ryan shook hands with Phil, then stalked briskly from the cubicle. Beth frowned as he walked past, watched to see if he'd make eye contact with her, but he didn't. She stayed with her father until he was taken off for his MRI scan, then went in search of Ryan. She needed to talk to him, to find out what he thought about her parents. Although, from what she'd seen, he didn't seem to have a problem with the fact that they were dwarfs, but did he have a problem when it came to dating her?

She knew the neuroses from her past were haunting her once again but she couldn't help it. Ryan was becoming more and more important to her and she needed to know whether he'd have a problem dating her…if, in fact, they ended up dating…given her family genetics. It was silly, stupid, but it was there, nevertheless. If he was going to hurt her, she'd be best to deal with it now, rather than later when she was completely in love with him.

Beth went to the orthopaedic department first, thinking he might have done some more paperwork, but the offices were dark and locked. Next she tried the ward but he wasn't there either. Her mother arrived and after she'd taken Isabelle to the MRI unit, Beth continued her search for Ryan, checking the ward once more.

Heather, the clinical nurse consultant, was sitting at the nurses' station when the phone rang. 'Orthopaedics.' Heather paused a moment, then nodded. 'She's here. Do you want to talk to her?'

Beth was surprised. A phone call for her already?

'OK. I'll send her down.' Heather replaced the receiver.

'Problem?' Beth asked, frowning.

'A and E's expecting an influx. Train derailment almost two hours ago. First few patients are about to arrive and the new dishy director of our department has requested that you join him.'

'Great. Just what I don't need.' It would also mean she wouldn't have the opportunity to speak to Ryan privately.

'Hey, don't complain. You get to work alongside him. I only get to drool whenever he comes in to do a ward round or check on the patients.'

Beth wondered whether she should say anything about her present living arrangements but decided against it for the moment. Now was not the time or the place. Besides, she knew exactly what sort of conclusions Heather would jump to and right now she wasn't in the mood for dealing with them. She said goodbye and headed to A and E, thinking about the kiss she and

Ryan had shared earlier that day. In that respect, Heather and anyone else who thought there might be more to their cohabitation would be right. She hit the button to release the doors into A and E, momentarily closing her eyes and shaking her head. How did she get herself into these situations? It wasn't as though she went hunting for a way to make her life as complicated as possible, but somehow it always seemed to happen.

'Snap to it, Dr Durant.' Ryan's brisk voice pierced through her thoughts and she opened her eyes to find him standing two feet away from her, pinning her with cold blue eyes. 'We've got incoming patients.'

Beth had had enough. She knew it wasn't good timing but there was one thing she wanted to get straight. Grabbing Ryan's arm, she pulled him into a nearby storeroom and closed the door.

'What?' He frowned at her. 'Beth?'

'Shut up, Ryan. Look, I don't know what your deal is or why you have this multiple personality disorder, but just drop it around me, OK?'

He folded his arms across his chest and listened indulgently, one eyebrow raised in surprise.

'I can't work properly wondering which person I'm going to be faced with,' she continued. 'Is it going to be the nice one or the one who's going to bite my head off? It doesn't promote a healthy working relationship, Ryan.'

'All this after only one week of working together? Pretty perceptive of you,' he countered.

'Last week actually wasn't so bad but after yesterday, when I was able to see what a genuinely nice person you are, I am now completely confused. Why do you do it?'

'Do what?'

'Try and hold yourself aloof. I'm not saying you should be flighty or footloose but just a real person with real emotions instead of being Dr Automaton. It's as though you can't relax at work in case you accidentally put a foot wrong. Well let me tell you that you're human both before and after you receive a knighthood…or at least that's what I've always imagined.'

There was silence between them for a moment, with Ryan staring down at her. 'Finished?'

Beth squared her shoulders. 'For now.'

He gave one nod and then turned towards the door. She reached out and stopped him, putting her hand over his. Both pulled back instantly, almost burnt from the touch. 'Ryan,' she said more softly, 'all I'm trying to say is just be yourself and not Sir Ryan, who's kind of a jerk sometimes.' She grimaced and shook her head. 'That came out wrong.'

'Yes. It did.'

This time, when he went to leave, she made no move to stop him. When he closed the door, she sighed. 'That went well.' She shook her head again and headed out, running slap bang into Tristan.

'Beth. What are you doing in the storeroom?' He frowned and looked over his shoulder at Ryan's retreating back before returning his attention to Beth. 'Didn't I just see Sir Ryan coming out of here?'

Beth groaned. 'We were talking.'

'Talking, eh? That's a new word for it.'

'Not now, Tris.'

'True. Now is definitely not the time. I heard about your dad, by the way. How's he doing?'

'Still having tests, as far as I know.' They started walking towards the nurses' station. 'It's bad this time. I think this might be it.'

'The wheelchair?'

'Yes.'

Tristan put his arm around Beth's shoulders and squeezed. 'You'll get through it. He'll be fine, Beth.'

'So everyone keeps telling me.' She sighed again, feeling a little more calm. She glanced at Ryan once more but he was engaged in a telephone conversation. 'So, do you know what we're going to be dealing with—train-accident-wise?'

'Haven't heard much. Just got the call to come in.'

'All hands, brace for impact,' she said, and Tristan smiled.

Ryan replaced the receiver and Beth turned to look at him. 'What's the news?'

'Your father's just finishing in MRI and Phil will come and find you when he has the results.'

Beth was stunned by Ryan's words. She'd thought he'd been on the phone regarding the train derailment yet he'd been checking up on her father. She frowned briefly, surprised by him once more.

'Er…thanks. I'll probably be in Theatre, knowing my luck.'

'Probably,' Ryan replied, and after giving her a brisk nod he walked away.

'That was weird.' Tristan watched their boss depart. 'There is something going on between the two of you, isn't there? If not, then he is definitely one strange guy.'

Beth closed her eyes, wondering whether she should say something or not, but after all Tristan was one of her closest friends. She opened her eyes and shrugged. 'It's nothing over the top or anything but we're kind of…sharing the same space.' She said the words softly.

'What?' Tristan's outburst surprised them both and she quickly shushed him.

'Nothing.' She forced a smile as they looked self-consciously at their colleagues. 'I'll tell you later,' she said between clenched teeth.

'Sorry,' he said. 'You caught me by surprise.'

'Let's talk about this later. Right now I'm going to go and change into theatre scrubs and then see if I can track down my mother. May as well be doing something useful while we're waiting for these ambulances.'

Tristan walked with her to the change rooms, apologising again for his outburst. 'What do you mean? You've piqued my curiosity.'

'We're both house-sitting for Marty and Natalie.'

Tristan's eyebrows shot up. 'You didn't know about this?'

'Nope. Neither did Ryan.'

'The newly-weds are matchmaking, eh?'

'Looks that way.'

'Is it working?'

They were outside the female change rooms and Beth merely rolled her eyes, punched in the code and walked away from him.

'I'll take that as a yes,' he called. A moment later he went into the male change rooms and was confronted by the man in question. 'Sir Ryan.'

'Tristan.'

They were both silent for a moment while Tristan pulled some theatre scrubs from the trolley. 'So, I hear you and Beth are both house-sitting.'

'Yes.'

'Nice and cosy.'

'Hmm.' Ryan frowned. He hardly knew Tristan, but Tristan definitely knew Beth so he decided to ask the question which had been bothering him for quite some time. 'Is she always so…infuriating?'

Tristan chuckled. 'Not usually, but it's good to see her expanding her boundaries, trying new things.'

'Why didn't she tell me about her parents sooner?'

'You mean about her dad's back?'

'Er…not exactly.'

'Ah, the dwarf issue. It's a big one for Beth. That doesn't mean it bothers her—I mean, they're her parents. They're all she's ever known but she's had to put up with a lot of spiteful people during school, and even med school, and if that wasn't enough, then came Jeff.'

'Ah…Jeff.'

'She's told you about him?' Tristan couldn't help the surprise he felt. 'Wow. That's big.'

Ryan shrugged. 'We were discussing bad relationships. His name came up.'

'It would. It happened a few years ago. They'd dated for a few months, things were getting serious. They were discussing marriage and then Jeff met her parents.'

'High-tailed it out of there?' Ryan guessed.

'Exactly.'

'So the strange dating habits?'

'Over-compensating. She'll ask a certain question to gauge a guy's reaction to people who are different. If they give the wrong answer, she doesn't bother with them again.'

'No second chances?'

'None.'

'She's trying to protect her parents,' Ryan said thoughtfully. 'And herself.'

'Anyone would protect the people they love from hurt, and as far as protecting herself, that's got nothing to do with her parents. She was well and truly hurt by that guy and it's always hard to let yourself trust again.'

'I know the feeling.'

'Then it appears you and Beth have something in common.'

'Quite a bit, really.' Ryan held his hand out to Tristan. 'Thanks.'

'Glad to help.' Tristan held Ryan's hand for a fraction of a second longer. 'Don't muck her around.'

'Noted.' Ryan headed out of the change rooms and back to A and E. He hated waiting around but at least he could now focus on his job rather than on the pretty blonde registrar who was sashaying towards him, the baggy green garments looking incredible on her.

'How's your mother holding up?' he asked.

'Just about to call her.' Beth called the MRI unit, hoping her father hadn't left there yet.

'No, they're still here,' she was told by the MRI consultant. 'Do you want to speak to your mother?'

'Thanks.' Beth waited for her mother.

'Beth?'

'How are you holding up, Mum?'

'Me? Oh, I'm fine, dear. Your dad's resting while they check the films.'

'Good.'

'Oh, and I must say, dear, that your new friend Arnold is such a wonderful man. Do you know, he gave me his card and told me to call him any time? Wasn't that sweet?'

'Very sweet.'

'He told me all about your adventures last night and how you and Ryan were cuddling to keep warm.'

'Terrific,' she replied blandly. 'Listen, Mum, there's been a train derailment and we're expecting quite a few casualties in pretty soon.'

'Oh, dear. Well, you go and do what you need to do and I'll speak to you later. I'll be fine.'

Beth closed her eyes, wishing she had the time to hear Phil's report, to be there when he explained the surgery and the possibility that her father might be permanently in a wheelchair. 'I love you, Mum.' Her voice choked as she said the words.

'I know, Beth. We'll be fine. We'll get through everything. We always have. Go and save some lives. That'll make your dad proud.'

Beth smiled. 'OK.' She rang off and turned, surprised to find Ryan still standing near her. She'd thought he'd gone to meet the ambulance.

'How's she doing?'

Beth shook her head sadly and sighed. 'She always knows the perfect thing to say to get me through whatever I need to get through.'

Ryan nodded. 'I have a mum like that.'

'Really?'

'Yes, and I've discovered that unfortunately they're a rare breed.' He smiled at her, not a smile that made her knees buckle but rather one that made her feel safe. It was a strange sensation. The entire day had been filled with strange sensations. He angled his head towards the incoming patients. 'Come on. Work time.'

CHAPTER NINE

THE next two to three hours passed in a blur as Beth and Ryan treated one patient after the next. A and E was busy, with beds lined up in the corridors. Triage Sister was almost tearing her hair out and extra staff were arriving to help out where necessary.

Beth stood at the scrub sink for the fourth time, having received the all-clear from the general surgeons who had just finished patching a young woman who'd received extensive abdominal injuries.

'Is Sir Ryan finished in Theatre?' Beth asked the scrub nurse.

'I'll check for you. Do you need him?'

Beth glanced away. Did she need him? That was certainly a loaded question. The attraction between them was becoming more and more desperate and at that moment she would have given anything just to be held by Ryan, to feel his strength seep into her to get her through the next few hours.

She nodded. 'If he's free,' she said, not looking at the nurse.

'I'll let you know.'

Beth closed her eyes for a moment, trying to find the strength to get herself under control. It had been such an emotionally draining day and she wasn't sure she would be able to find her professional self once more. 'But you will,' she whispered, and sighed.

'You will what?' came Ryan's deep voice from behind her.

Startled, Beth quickly glanced over her shoulder. 'Scrub Nurse was just trying to reach you.'

'Need help?' He crossed to the scrub sink.

'Yes, please.'

Without another word he switched on the taps and began to scrub. 'Tired?'

'Yes.'

'We're almost done.'

She acknowledged his words with a nod. 'How'd your last patient go?' She glanced at him and watched as he swallowed.

'Died on the table.'

Beth slumped her shoulders and shook her head, knowing exactly how he felt. It was never easy to lose a patient and especially when you were in an operating theatre, working hard to save that person's life. They'd both seen death countless times and it wouldn't change any time in the near future but, still, every death affected you in one way or another. Their training had taught them to pigeonhole their emotions and move on, and that's exactly what they would do now.

'What's the situation with this next patient?' he asked after a moment.

'Elise Cartwright, aged nineteen. Extensive abdominal injuries and the general surgical registrar said she's fractured her pelvis.'

'X-rays?'

'In Theatre. Personally, I'd prefer three-dimensional CT scans to see exactly where the fracture is but according to the general reg. there are bony fragments which need to be seen to immediately.'

'Let's get that organised, then. Any other injuries?'

'Fractured tibia, which we can fix by open reduction and internal fixation. I can do that. I just really wanted you here for the pelvic exploration.'

'Patch her up for tonight and check her out in a few days' time?'

'I think so.'

Ryan nodded and glanced at her, giving her a tired smile. 'Sounds like a plan.'

'Always good to have a plan.'

He paused for a moment before clearing his throat and saying in a quieter voice, 'Any news on your dad?'

'Yes. Phil said he'll operate tomorrow morning when all the test results are back. Last report was that Mum was over in the residential wing and Dad was sleeping.'

'Good to hear.' Another beat, then, 'You're all right to operate?'

'Yes.'

'Want me to take the lead?'

Beth looked up at him with a tired smile. 'Yes,' she said again. 'If it's not too much trouble.'

'It's fine.' He smiled again and this time it had the effect of renewing her and giving her energy to continue. Her body went all tingly and she shook her head in bemusement.

'You have no idea how high voltage your smile is, do you?'

As Ryan's eyes widened, Beth realised she'd spoken the words out loud. 'Uh…no. No, I guess I don't.'

'I'm sorry,' she said, and hung her head. 'My brain is so fried I have no idea when I'm just thinking or talking out loud.'

'Beth?' She lifted her head and looked at him. 'I'm glad I make you feel that way.'

'You are?'

He nodded and smiled again. This time she laughed and shook her head. 'OK. You've revitalised me so let's get to Theatre before the effects of your smiles wear off and I fall to the floor in a puddle of exhaustion.'

'What a good idea.' He felt just as revitalised by her words as she was by his smiles.

The operation on Elise was long and intricate but eventually both were satisfied with her status. Once they'd sorted out the mess of her pelvis, they set to work and performed the open reduction and internal fixation on Elise's right tibia.

'She's a very fortunate woman,' Ryan told Elise's parents once the operation had been completed. 'Dr Durant and I would like her to have further X-rays regarding her pelvic fracture and hopefully, by this time next week, we'll have a better idea of whether we need to fix the fractures invasively or whether they'll heal better by themselves.'

'Is that common?'

'Yes. Pelvic fractures need time to settle,' Beth replied. 'Once we do the scans tomorrow, we'll have a better idea, but for now she's stable and should be out of Recovery soon. You'll be able to see her then.'

'Thank you so much.' Mr Cartwright shook their hands in gratitude. When they left, Ryan took one look at Beth and took her to the doctors' tearoom.

'You stay here and I'll go check the situation with Triage Sister. Although last time I spoke to her, things were gradually returning to normal...whatever that means.'

'Normal in a hospital? Isn't that an oxymoron?'

Ryan smiled and headed out. Beth sat and put her feet up and her head back, and closed her eyes. Every muscle in her body ached and as far as she was concerned, she could have stayed right there and slept for the next ten hours straight.

'Hey.'

Beth opened her eyes and was surprised to see Ryan standing beside her. 'I thought you were going to speak to Triage Sister?'

'I did.' He smiled. 'I've been gone for about fifteen minutes.' He placed his hand gently beneath her neck. 'Sit up, Beth, or you're going to get a bad crick in your neck.'

'I think it's already there.' She winced slightly as she sat up straighter.

Ryan sat down beside her. 'How are you holding up?'

Beth shrugged. 'Apart from the exhaustion? Not bad.'

'But not good, right?'

She smiled tiredly at him. 'I need to check on Dad and then I think I'll head home...er...well, back to Nat and Marty's.'

Ryan returned her smile, his blue eyes twinkling. 'I knew what you meant.' Their gazes held and the smiles slowly disappeared, to be replaced by looks of intense hunger. Neither of them moved but at the same time they seemed to draw closer together. It was as though they were inhabiting each other's comfort zones and yet it was still very comfortable...not invasive at all. Beth marvelled at the way this man made her feel. Safe, secure and—above all—protected. She wasn't sure what he protected her from...perhaps it was loneliness, perhaps it was from feeling insecure about herself. She didn't know and right now she didn't care.

She sighed and reached her hand out to him, only to find his hand was already there, waiting for hers. When they touched she gasped, the contact sending a thrill of delight through her before she relaxed once more, content in the knowledge that the delight was mutually shared.

The door to the tearoom opened and both jerked their hands apart. Ryan got to his feet. He stalked over to the coffee-machine as Joey walked in.

'There you are, Beth. I was looking for you. Good job on that last patient.'

'Thanks.' Beth glanced at Ryan as he poured himself a cup of coffee. Why had he moved so quickly? Had he just been startled? This wasn't the first time they'd been interrupted and each time he seemed to react the same way. At the wedding he'd been on his feet immediately and moving as far away from her as possible.

'So.' Joey sat down in the seat Ryan had just vacated. 'Are you heading home now?'

'Soon.'

He nodded. 'If you need a lift, I'd be more than happy to give you one.'

Beth was surprised for a moment. 'Well…I wanted to check on my parents and also just make sure my patients are doing all right before I leave.' She looked Ryan's way again, hoping he'd step in and say something…she wasn't sure what but right now she didn't have the brain power to deal with Joey. Then again, with the way Ryan had moved like lightning, perhaps she shouldn't count on him coming to her rescue. Heaven forbid if anyone at the hospital thought they might actually be friends…let alone have any other feelings towards each other.

'That's all right,' Joey was saying. 'I'm happy to wait.'

'Joey. It's two o'clock in the morning.'

'So? I'm awake…you're awake.'

'I wouldn't count on that too much. My eyelids feel very heavy.'

'All the more reason for me to drive you home.' He reached across and patted her knee. The touch helped to clear some of the cotton wool from Beth's mind.

'I'll *bet*,' Ryan said, clearing his throat, 'that you wouldn't mind giving me a lift home either.'

Bet? Beth frowned for a moment before she twigged to what Ryan was saying. That's right. Joey had been one of the men who'd made that bet. Was he trying to collect?

'You didn't bring your car?' Joey asked, a little puzzled at Ryan's attitude.

'No. I was with Beth when she received the phone call about her father and we headed straight to the airport.' Ryan's words were clear and concise and Joey's confusion suddenly cleared.

'You were with Beth?' The anaesthetist looked from one to the other. Beth simply stared at Ryan.

'Yes. We're together.'

Beth's jaw was now hanging open in total shock. He'd done it. The man was a constant source of surprise. Just when she thought he'd deny having anything to do with her, there he was, making a declaration.

Joey, completely stunned, turned to look at Beth. She quickly closed her mouth. 'Is this why you haven't been doing your usual dating thing since your return?' He didn't seem too annoyed or put out, merely amazed.

'It's been a hectic time, what with Natalie's wedding and all.'

Joey snapped his fingers. 'Of course. I keep forgetting the connection you two have. You're Natalie's friend and you're Marty's cousin.' He stood and put his hands in his pockets. 'You were both at their wedding and that's why you've got to know each other so quickly.' He shrugged, then smiled at them both. 'A lot of the women in the hospital will be sorry to hear this news. Still…' He took his hands out and rubbed them together. 'All the more for the rest of us bachelors. Well, I'll leave you to see Beth home, then, Ryan.' Another goofy smile at them both before he headed out of the room.

Beth simply stared at the closed door for a moment, amazed

at what had transpired in such a short time. Then she looked over to where Ryan was leaning against the bench, watching her. 'Huh.'

'What does that mean?' he asked a little cautiously.

She wasn't sure herself. In one way she was ecstatic Ryan had said something, and in another she was disheartened that Joey had given up so easily. She shook her head, trying to put the past few minutes into perspective, but couldn't. She was so flummoxed she wasn't quite sure what to say.

'I think I'll go check on my father.' She stood, surprised her legs were able to support her weight. Ryan tossed the rest of his coffee in the sink and quickly washed the cup.

'I'll come with you.'

'Really? Why? To cement the gossip you can bet has already started?'

'You're annoyed? With me?'

Beth opened her mouth to speak but her mind was too fuzzy to put her feelings into words. 'No. Yes. Oh, I don't know.' She sighed and shook her head. 'I'm tired and I just want to get to bed. I promise to argue about any topic you want but only after I've had some sleep.'

Ryan shook his head and smiled, coming over and taking her hand in his. 'Let's go check on your dad *and* cement the gossip.'

'You're sure?'

His answer was to smile and tug her out the door.

Beth had never felt more self-conscious in her life and was glad it was the early hours of the morning, meaning the hospital corridors were deserted. But the people they passed definitely did double-takes. When they arrived at the high-dependency ward, Ryan dropped her hand and let her go and check on her father alone while he waited with the nurses.

As she walked up to the bed, she realised her father was awake. 'Hi,' she whispered, and kissed his forehead. 'How are you feeling?'

'Doped up.'

She smiled. 'No pain?' She took his hand in hers and held it tightly.

'I'm doing nicely.'

'Good. Is Mum over in the residential wing?'

'That's what the sister told me.'

'Good,' she said again.

'How about you? Tough night in Theatre?'

'It was busy.'

'You're tired, pet. Go home and rest. Your mother was telling me all about Ryan and how he's Marty's cousin and the fun you two had the other night.'

'I'd hardly call assisting at an accident site "fun", Dad.'

Daniel smiled. 'That's my girl.' He squeezed her hand. 'I'm ever so proud of you, pet.'

Beth felt tears begin to mist her eyes. 'I know, Dad.'

'You're such a wonderful daughter and we love you very much.'

The lump in her throat was getting bigger by the second. She leaned over and kissed his forehead again, not letting go of his hand. 'I love you, too, Dad.' She sniffed. 'And right now you need to get some rest or else Sister's going to restrict my visiting if she thinks I'm going to upset her patients.'

'I'm not upset, pet, just telling it like it is.'

Beth met his gaze and nodded, knowing he was talking about his condition. 'Things are changing.'

'We'll make it. Phil's a good doctor. He'll do his best.'

Beth nodded.

'Go home, pet. Get some sleep and I'll do the same.'

'OK.' She bit her lip, desperately trying to hold back the tears as she kissed him again. 'Don't be too difficult for the staff,' she said with a forced smile.

'Now, where's the fun in that?'

The smile turned genuine. ''Night, Dad.' Swallowing over the lump in her throat once more, she headed back to the nurses' station where Ryan was sitting in a chair, his head forward and eyes closed.

'Everything all right?' he asked, not moving. Beth reached past him for a tissue and blew her nose.

'He's good.' She hiccuped a few times as she breathed in, and Ryan opened his eyes.

'Are you all right?'

'Just a little emotional. He looks so…frail lying there.'

Ryan stood and took her hand again. 'Let's check on our patients and then we can get out of here. I've ordered a taxi to be waiting outside the hospital in twenty minutes. It's not Arnold,' he said as they left the HD unit. 'The man doesn't need to be disturbed at this hour of night just to ferry us home.'

Beth grinned. 'That is his job, Ryan, but I know what you mean.' Twenty minutes later they were both in their own clothes and coats and standing outside the hospital, where the taxi was waiting for them.

Ryan climbed into the back with her and after they'd put their seat belts on, he pulled her into his arms. She gave in to the need to sleep and snuggled up to him, closing her eyes. The next thing she knew, they were outside Marty's house. Ryan paid the driver and put his arm around her for support as they walked up to the house, the sensor light blinding them both once more.

'That light's a nuisance,' Ryan muttered as he unlocked the door. 'This is the second time in as many nights that I've brought you home dead-dog tired.'

Beth smiled as she walked in. 'And I thank you, kind sir.'

'You're most welcome, m'lady.' He kicked the door shut with his foot, wanting desperately to pull her into his arms. Instead, he placed his hand tenderly beneath her elbow and guided her towards her room. She went in and kicked her shoes off. Ryan stayed in the doorway, keeping his distance.

'You sleep tight,' he said, and turned to go.

'Wait.'

He pivoted on his heel, raising his eyebrows questioningly.

Beth yawned and walked back towards him. 'Do I get a goodnight kiss?'

'You're getting punchy again.'

'And what if I am? The hospital knows we're together so I think I'm at least entitled to a goodnight kiss.'

'I thought we agreed to argue about this later.'

'Who's arguing? I'm just asking for a little kiss.'

Ryan shook his head but still didn't enter her bedroom. It was as though there was an invisible force field keeping him out, yet he knew if he crossed the threshold he would want a lot more than just a few goodnight kisses. His passion for Beth was increasing with every passing second and it was his sole motivation for saying what he had earlier. The thought of Beth even considering going home with Joey had made his blood boil.

Now she was asking him to kiss her, which was what he'd been wanting to do for quite some time. Was he strong enough to refuse? He watched as she slowly made her way towards him and he groaned as his need for her increased. Did she have any idea just how incredibly beautiful she was? As much as he wanted to fight the attraction, he knew he was fighting a losing battle and when she stood in front of him and lifted her hand to gently caress his face, Ryan felt any remaining strength he had crumble.

Her fingers worked their way into his hair and he closed his eyes, relishing the way she made him feel. Rising on tiptoe, she lifted her chin, her hands urging his head down so their lips could meet.

It was a sweet, tender kiss, both taking their time to familiarise themselves once more with the minute sensations each could evoke. He hadn't rushed her the last time they'd kissed and he didn't intend to rush now. She was exhausted, yet the feel of his warm lips on hers gave her a feeling of pure contentment.

His lips were so soft on hers, their tenderness helping emotions she'd had no idea she could feel rise to the surface. His breath, warm and mingling with hers only added to the mix, his scent wrapping itself around her, drawing her in.

She opened her mouth to deepen the kiss but Ryan lifted his hands to encircle her wrists and gently pulled back, holding her hands in his. He gazed down into her face and couldn't resist pressing one more kiss to her luscious lips before taking a step back and letting her hands go.

'We need to sleep.'

'Mmm,' she sighed, and closed her eyes, swaying slightly.

'We have a busy morning schedule. First arguing, then operating, then clinic.'

She smiled. 'Sounds like fun.' She opened her eyes, peering at him beneath her heavy lashes.

'Go to sleep, Beth.'

She nodded, unable to speak. Ryan called on all his strength to walk away, and a moment later he heard her door close. There, she was safely behind a closed door. He walked through the dark house, picking up the real estate agent's listing off the bench and switching on the heating.

He needed to move out of Marty's house…and fast, because Beth was becoming way too addictive.

CHAPTER TEN

THE next morning, Beth woke from the most delicious sleep she'd had in a long time. She smiled and stretched, trying to recall exactly what it was that had put her in this mood. It was then she remembered her goodnight kiss from Ryan…or had that been part of the dream? She frowned for a moment before convincing herself it had been very real.

Either way, her alarm was beeping, which meant she had to get out of bed. With great reluctance she flipped back the bedcovers and slipped her feet into her ugg boots and pulled on her dressing-gown. Smothering a yawn, she headed out to the kitchen in search of coffee…and found Ryan instead.

She stopped, watching him for a second, unsure of what to say or how to act. Her mouth went dry as she felt her limbs unable to move. He was mesmerising and he was only preparing the coffee. Right now he had his back to her and thankfully he was wearing a shirt. A pang of regret passed through her and she realised that she'd much rather see his bare chest again. Still, she supposed it was good that he was doing his best to adhere to the rules they'd set down. As yesterday, a pair of denims rode his hips and his large feet were bare.

Yummy, was the thought that came into her mind and she knew exactly what she wanted for breakfast. Startled at her own thoughts, she began to blush. She couldn't help it. The man brought out aspects of her personality she'd never known existed.

When he finally turned and saw her, she gulped. His shirt was unbuttoned and hung open to reveal his washboard stomach. She worked very hard not to lick her lips and swallowed a few times, trying to get control over her senses.

'Beth.' He flicked the coffee-machine on. 'Hi. I didn't hear you.' He followed her gaze and quickly began buttoning up the shirt, cutting off the view. 'Sorry. I forgot.' He shrugged nonchalantly. 'Then again, I love it when you look at me that way.'

Her gaze flicked up to meet his as a wave of heat washed over her body at his words. She opened her mouth to speak but no words came out and she forced herself to look away from him. Why did he say such things to her? She'd just started getting herself under control and then he went and undid it all by saying something like that. It had to stop.

As she searched wildly for something to say, Ryan filled the void. 'You look all cosy and sleep-tousled. Why don't you sit down and let me get you breakfast?'

Breakfast? How was she supposed to consume food when her throat felt thick with repressed desire? Still, she shuffled around the other side of the bench and sat down on one of the stools.

'You don't have to cook for me, you know.' Finally she managed to find her voice.

'Cooking relaxes me.'

'You need relaxing? It's first thing in the morning. You're supposed to be bright-eyed and bushy-tailed.'

'I didn't sleep well,' he muttered. 'So…cereal or toast?'

'Wow. You are a real gourmet.'

He smiled at her words, surprised that just a few minutes in her company had improved his disposition no end. She looked so cuddly, all wrapped up, and he was positive she didn't realise her hair was all mussed and sticking out slightly. It was just as he'd imagined it…*vividly* imagined it.

'Well, for starters, the coffee's on. Here, let me get you a glass of juice.' He quickly turned and opened the fridge, pulling out the juice then a glass and pouring it for her. He handed it over and when she drank the entire glass in one go, he raised his eyebrows in surprise.

'Feel better?'

'A little more awake but not better.'

He smiled again. 'OK. You can have cereal *and* toast if you'd prefer but, given that we've got a lot to get through this morning, I wasn't sure we had time for a cooked breakfast.'

Beth's eyes widened a little. 'What do we have to get through this morning?' She hoped it had something to do with his mouth on hers.

'Arguing. Remember?'

'Oh.' She tried not to show her disappointment. 'Arguing. That's right.'

He put both hands on the bench and leaned forward. 'You want to go first?'

He'd showered, she realised. His hair was still slightly damp and the freshness from his shower clung to him in such a potent way she was struck dumb. She met his gaze and once more felt the control he held over her. If she edged across the bench, their lips would meet, and she was positive it was what they both wanted more than any type of food. 'Me? Uh… OK. I'll go…um…first.' She cleared her throat. 'I'll…er…have toast, please.'

He smiled and straightened. 'I meant the arguing.' He took out some bread and put it in the toaster.

'Well, what if I can't remember what I wanted to argue about?'

'Does it matter? We're scheduled for arguing.'

'So you live your life solely by schedule?'

'Yes. As a matter of fact, I do. Besides…' He leaned across the bench again, but this time he brought his face within kissing distance. Beth gulped, her lips parting in anticipation, her heart pounding wildly against her chest. 'After we argue, I have time scheduled for us to kiss and make up.'

Her breath came out in a rush as she simply stared at him, his face, his mouth so close to her own. 'Can't we skip the arguing?'

A slow smile touched his lips and when he spoke, his breath fanned across her. 'Are you requesting a change to the schedule?' The vibrations from his deep voice rumbled through her and she flicked her gaze up to meet his.

'Would it be so bad? After all, it's what we both want.'

He looked at her mouth, so close, so sweet. 'True.'

'Or we could make up before *and* after the scheduled arguing,' she offered.

Ryan tilted his head to the side, drawing even closer to her. 'I like the way you think, Dr Durant.'

The agonising second it took for the remaining distance between them to be closed made her almost hyperventilate with longing. This was their third kiss and she sincerely hoped it was also only the first one for the day. At some point yesterday they'd seemed to have crossed a boundary where the attraction started taking precedence over everything else that was going on in their lives. Yet right now she wanted this moment to speed up and slow down at the same time.

'I had a dream about you last night,' she told him, her eyes fluttering closed as their noses touched.

'Hmm?'

'You were…standing very close to me, your arms were around me and you were gazing down into my eyes with the most incredible expression of wonder.' Her words were choppy and punctuated with little sighs of longing, prolonging the sweet torture. 'It was as though you'd unwrapped a big, shiny present and didn't have a clue what to do with it.'

'I had the same dream.' He shifted, gently rubbing his freshly shaved cheek alongside hers as he dipped his head to nuzzle her neck. She moved to accommodate him, marvelling at his words. 'In my dream, though, I knew exactly what to do with my shiny present.'

'Oh,' she sighed, and brought her hands up to bury them in his hair, the dampness only reminding her of how fresh this attraction between the two of them was. 'Did you? Well, why don't you show me?'

'Hmm.'

She opened her eyes slightly and saw that small smile touch his lips once more. The sight made her melt and her hands guided his head so their lips could find each other. An urgency she'd never felt before ripped through her and she knew that if he didn't kiss her, and soon, she might suffocate from longing. 'Ryan…' she whispered impatiently. 'I'm burning up for you.'

His breathing was as hard and as furious as hers when he eventually pressed his mouth eagerly to her lips.

The hunger, the heat, the all consuming power they had over each other flowed through both of them as their pent-up desires and frustration poured out. Where their previous kisses had been more of an exploratory nature, this one was all primal, both seeking and securing the responses they desired.

Never before had a woman responded to him so ardently as Beth did, and Ryan wanted nothing more than to have her body pressed close to his. Still bracing his hands on the benchtop, he shifted his weight and clambered over the obstacle keeping him apart from Beth, his lips pressed firmly on hers the entire time.

Sitting on the bench, he manoeuvred his legs so they were on either side of the stool she still sat on. Now that he could gather her close, he deepened the kiss, his arms holding her firmly as they continued their eager onslaught.

Beth knew she had to breathe but right now she had other things on her mind, such as giving and taking in equal amounts from the man before her. Her hands slipped down from his head and under his arms. Down, down, they travelled until they found the end of his shirt. Unable to resist, she slipped her hands beneath the fabric to touch the contours of his torso.

'Beth.' Her name was a guttural groan torn from his lips as her fingers travelled first up the front of his perfect body before slipping around to the back, her nails gently scratching. Again Ryan groaned and lifted her slightly, pressing her chest as close to his as he could.

Their mouths, their minds, their bodies…all were totally in sync and Beth had never experienced such a powerful sensation before. It was scary and exciting all at the same time and all she was really conscious of was that she wanted those sensations to go on and on for ever.

It couldn't be.

The thought came from somewhere deep within her and she hated the fact that some negative thought had broken through the barrier of the emotions.

The check-list. The check-list.

With an agonising moan Beth pulled back, panting. She looked up at Ryan but his eyes were still closed, his mouth still affected from her touch. She leaned weakly against him, his arms holding her firmly.

'You all right?' he whispered.

'Mmm-hmm.' That was all the answer she was capable of. Her check-list. How could she have forgotten her check-list? It was how she'd lived her life—as far as men were concerned—since Jeff had hurt her. She couldn't throw that all away because Ryan kissed like a dream, making her forget all rational thought!

'Wow!'

'Yeah, wow,' she echoed, not wanting to let him go, although the longer she stood there, holding him so tightly, the harder it was to actually move away. Ryan didn't seem to be in any great rush to release her and so she stayed where she was, letting her breathing return to normal. Reality was also starting to creep into her thoughts and she reluctantly allowed it.

'Can we, please, get this arguing out of the way so we can get back to the making up because I gotta tell you, Beth, if this is how we make up, I'm going to be picking fights with you all day long.'

It was exactly what she wanted and didn't want to hear. Still, she pulled back and looked up at him with a smile, her eyes still glazed with desire. He pressed one quick kiss to her lips before releasing his hold on her. As her own hands slipped down his back, he gave a shudder of delight and again she marvelled at the power she seemed to hold over him.

He took both her hands in his and held them for a moment before kissing each one. 'Breakfast.'

'Arguing,' she countered, and by mutual consent they moved at the same time—Ryan sliding back across the bench and Beth shifting her stool and sitting down more comfortably.

'So, what's first on the list?' he asked as he tossed away the toast, which was now cold. He put two more pieces of bread in the toaster and, after wiping the bench, poured two cups of coffee.

'The arguing list?'

'Yes.'

Beth racked her brains.

'Come on, honey. You've got to think of something because we have a lot of making up to do, remember?'

Beth smiled at him again, then nodded. 'OK. Why did you tell Joey we were together?'

'Instead of telling him we were just house-sitting the same house?'

'Yes.'

'That's hardly an argument, Beth.'

'I can make it one,' she said pointedly, as he dodged the question.

Ryan smiled at her, then shrugged. 'I didn't want him to think he stood a chance with you.'

'But that's got nothing to do with you.'

'The fact that you might date some other guy when all I can think about is kissing you is nothing to do with me? I beg to differ.'

'Oh. Hmm. I see your point, but you know everyone at the hospital will think we're…' She gestured with her hand. 'You know…'

'Sleeping together? Having sex?' He grinned as she blushed and again he just wanted to press his mouth to hers. She was so adorable when she became flustered and he was starting to think up ways to get her flustered more often.

'Yes.'

'So?'

'So we're not.'

'But we could.'

'But we won't. Ryan, this thing…whatever it is between us

is too confusing, and adding sex to the mix would make it even more so.'

'Because both of us have dated colleagues before and been burnt.'

'It makes it more difficult for us to trust our hearts to someone else.'

The toast popped up and Ryan took it out, handing her a piece and getting the jam from the fridge. She had to wait until he'd spread his toast and taken another good long sip of his coffee before he made any comment.

'You've got that right. Trust. A tricky thing and not easy to do.'

'Geraldine really hurt you.'

'We've covered the fact that she ripped my heart out—twice.'

'But there's more to it than that.'

'There always is.'

'Will you tell me about the second time?'

'The time when I should have known better?'

Beth nodded.

'I was doing my final orthopaedic rotation in Melbourne and she was working as a neurosurgical registrar. At first I kept things strictly business but I don't think I'd fully recovered from the first time she'd torn my heart out so was a willing victim to have her do it again.'

'Masochist,' Beth teased.

'We became friends again and before I knew it we were dating once again. This time, though, she was more subtle in her manipulations. She had the financial freedom from her father but he was still a heavy influence in her life. She would say it didn't matter how much I earned, that she didn't care, but when we started talking marriage once more, she showed her true colours yet again. I couldn't believe I'd been such a fool to fall for the same act twice.

'This time, though, I confronted her on the issue of money and why on earth we needed to have so much when we already had more than enough. That's when she told me that money was no longer enough. She needed prestige. Her father wanted her to invent something, a new technique, a breakthrough, *anything* which would ensure her name lived on in the history books for ever.'

'And caring for her patients? That wasn't enough prestige?'

'That's what I thought at the time. I realised it wasn't going to work out between us…*again*. This time when I tried to break it off, she let me have it with both barrels. She tore me down, she belittled me, told me I was worthless to her and her career as I'd never amount to anything. I was just ordinary. Now I know the saying "Sticks and stones may break my bones but names will never hurt me" is supposed to make you feel better, but it didn't.'

Beth nodded, knowing exactly what he meant. 'What she said really hurt.'

'Yes.'

'It caused your heart to rip in two. All the love and trust you'd given had been abused.'

'Yes.'

'But, worst of all, she made you question yourself.'

'Yes.'

'Your morals, your ethics.'

'Exactly.' How could Beth understand him so well? 'I needed to get away, not only from her but from the rest of the system. Medicine isn't about making lots of money, it's about helping people, and I realised that the group of so-called friends I'd surrounded myself with were much more interested in the former than the latter.'

'Off to join an aid organisation?'

'That's where I found people with the dedication I felt our profession required. It was also where I witnessed one horror after another. Then I went to London and surprisingly received a knighthood. Two weeks after the ceremony, Geraldine turned up.'

'Oh?'

'She wanted to pick up where we'd left off and I, naturally, wanted nothing to do with her.'

'She was in love with the knighthood?'

Ryan shook his head with veiled amusement. 'She couldn't understand why I wanted nothing to do with her and would casually turn up at functions I was attending and always managed to be sitting next to me when the photographers were around. She started rumours around the hospital that we were dating again, touting herself as the long-lost love of my life.'

'If she couldn't earn her own place in the medical history books, she'd marry it?'

'Something like that. I threw myself into my work and took on more responsibility than I was probably ready for. Now I can't seem to get rid of it.'

Beth nodded. 'That explains why you try to separate those two parts of your life.'

'Ah…next thing to argue about. Your little speech in the storeroom.'

She grimaced. 'I'm sorry, Ryan. I was tired, I was emotional about my father.' She gasped. 'My Dad!' She brushed the crumbs off her hands and went to the phone, dialling the hospital. 'See what you do to me? You make me forget everything—even my own father.'

'He slept well. I've already checked.'

She was surprised again at his caring. 'Really?'

He shrugged as though it were nothing. 'I told you, I had a restless night.'

'Well…thank you for checking on him.'

'You're welcome.' He smiled at her and again rational thought seemed to disappear as her gaze flicked from his eyes to his mouth. Then her call was connected and she turned her attention to it. A few minutes later she was sitting back on her stool, having spoken to her mother and received an update from the ward sister.

'Now. Sorry. We were discussing my outburst in the storeroom yesterday.'

'That's right. More toast?'

'Yes, thanks.' She sipped at her coffee. 'I had no right to say those things to you.'

'I think you did and actually, on reflection, it was nice to hear them. It shows me that you're not…' He shrugged, feeling a little self-conscious.

'Interested in the knighthood?'

'Exactly.'

'Why do you let it change you?'

He frowned at her question. 'I don't change. I'm still a dedicated doctor.'

'I don't dispute that, Ryan. It's your attitude towards your staff. It's as though you feel you need to play the part, as though you feel you didn't deserve the knighthood and now you need to live up to some imaginary expectations. If your staff find out you're human, they might not respect you and *they* may start to think you don't deserve it.'

Ryan was stunned. He couldn't believe she was saying these things to him. The scary thing was, she was one hundred per cent correct. It was exactly how he thought, how he felt and why he held himself aloof. He hadn't realised he'd been changing, but he had.

'I'm sorry,' she said, watching the reactions cross his face. 'There I go again. I only open my mouth to change feet.'

He handed her a piece of toast, then excused himself. Beth closed her eyes, wishing she'd just kept quiet, but on the other hand this was their scheduled time to argue. She looked over her shoulder in the direction he'd just gone. Did this mean their making-up session was off?

He returned a moment later with something in his hands. He handed her a velvet-covered box. 'What's this?' Beth ran her fingertips across the plush surface.

'Open it.'

She did and then gasped, gazing down at the award inside. 'This is the insignia of your knighthood?'

'Yes.'

She studied it for a moment before looking back up at him, delight in her eyes. 'You should be proud of it, Ryan.'

'But do I deserve it? I only did what I needed to do to make my life easier, to make my patients' lives easier.'

'You cared.'

'I'm a doctor. It's what I do. Thousands of doctors around the world do their part. They care, they invent things.'

'And, you never know, they might receive a knighthood one day.'

'Geraldine set the whole thing up.' The words were said with bleakness and Beth reached out and took his hand in hers. 'Somehow she learned of my work overseas, the device and technique I'd invented, and her father is very influential in those circles.'

'That still doesn't mean anything. Your name was put forward. That's all. An independent committee decides who gets what and honestly, Ryan, what does it matter? If you keep viewing the knighthood as some sort of harbinger of doom, then Geraldine is still winning. Don't give her the satisfaction. Just accept the situation and move on.'

'Is that what you do?'

'Meaning?'

'Your parents.'

'My parents?' She withdrew her hand.

'You used to crazy-date because you were looking for the guy who will accept your parents. You ask very carefully worded questions and if the poor guy doesn't pass the test, you move on.'

Her gaze darkened. 'You've been talking to Tristan.'

'He told me a bit more about Jeff.'

'Did he now? So glad I could be the topic of your locker-room conversations.'

'Hey, I belong to the heart-ripped-out club, too, remember. I know what it's like.'

'Oh, sure. You know what it's like to have lived with a prejudice against you for your entire life? You know what it's like to have kids at school laugh at your parents because they're taller than them? You know what it's like to have teenage boys refusing to go out with you in case they catch some sort of germ?' Tears gathered in her eyes. 'And then, after many years of being careful, I make yet another bad decision by trusting a man, thinking that he loved me, yet when he met my parents, I saw it there in his eyes. The shock, the fear—the unspoken question that if we were to get married and have children, would they be like their grandparents?'

She sniffed. 'That was the reason Jeff left. He couldn't stand the thought of having children who weren't "normal". That's why I started the standard-dating. That's why I'd ask my questions, and if those men mentioned anything about anyone with a disability, they were off the list. To become a mother one day is something that is very important to me, and I need to find a man who doesn't care about appearance but is able to love with his heart, no matter what.'

The tears were now flowing slowly down her cheeks and she jumped from the stool and headed into her bedroom, growling at the clock as she realised the time. She held on to the tears until she was beneath the spray of the shower, letting the water wash away her pain and torment. Hard on the heels of those volatile emotions came the realisation that Ryan was a lot further along her check-list than she'd realised. In fact, with the way he was showing such genuine concern for her parents, it looked as though that, too, might get crossed off.

'But you've just thrown him the bonus question,' she told herself as she towelled herself dry and started to dress. Would he be prepared to marry her and have children, knowing she carried the same genes as her parents? Personally, she had no problem with the concept and the chances were extremely slim. It all depended on who she married and their genealogy, but she didn't want to explain that to Ryan now. She needed him desperately to pull through this important challenge.

'And why?' she asked as she glared at her reflection in the mirror. 'Because you've already fallen in love with him. You fool.'

CHAPTER ELEVEN

WHEN she emerged from her bedroom, Beth had her professional mask in place. Make-up hid her red eyes and the suit she wore was the severest one she owned. Professional—it was the only way she was going to get through this day.

Ryan walked towards her, jangling his keys in one hand, briefcase in the other. He was dressed in a business suit as well. 'Ready to go?'

'Yes, thanks.'

'We can take Marty's four-wheel-drive.'

She nodded, not in the mood to argue. If they didn't leave soon, they would both be late and she knew how much Ryan disliked being late. She collected her bag and followed him through the house to the laundry door, which led to the garage.

He unlocked the car and held her door open. 'Need help getting in?'

Beth eyed the step up and realised that wearing a skirt today had been a mistake. Still, no time to change. She nodded and held out her hand. Ryan helped her in, both of them glancing at each other at the merest of touches, feeling the burning attraction that pumped through their veins.

When she was in, Ryan opened the garage door and walked round to climb in the driver's side. Neither of them spoke much on the ride and by the time they arrived at the hospital Beth felt she had her emotions under control. She knew people would see them arriving together and she didn't care. She knew they'd be gossiped about today and, again, she didn't care. Things in the past seemed so trivial compared to how she was feeling this morning.

She was in love with Ryan Cooper and she wasn't at all sure she was happy about it.

After he'd parked in the doctors' car park, he undid his seat belt and turned to face her. 'Just a minute, Beth. There's something I want to say.'

She shifted slightly to look at him better. Expecting him to speak, she was unprepared when he leaned across and placed a lingering kiss on her lips, soft and sweet. Her eyelids fluttered closed as her mouth moved automatically beneath his. Their programming was right, they were completely compatible, yet there were still doubts…not only in her but she also felt it in him.

When he pulled back, she whispered, 'What was that for?'

'Just fulfilling my schedule. We needed to make up, remember? After our argument.'

'Oh.' Beth frowned, a little bewildered by the man.

He took her hand in his. 'Look, I'm sorry if I said things to hurt you before.'

'I'm sorry, too,' she replied but he placed a finger tenderly over her lips, silencing her.

'We still have so much to work through but I think we deserve to give ourselves the chance to try.'

She nodded and kissed his fingertip. Ryan groaned and pulled his hand away.

'And don't do things like that because you make me forget everything else. I've never been so frustrated in all my life. Work has never been so hard to focus on before, but when you're around I find it hard to concentrate on anything but you.'

Beth gasped at his words, her eyes as wide as saucers.

'So if I'm a bit stand-offish today or come across as my alter ego, please, don't take it personally. I'm just trying to get through the day.'

Beth bit her lip, not sure how she was supposed to respond. 'OK.'

'Good.' With that, he opened the door and climbed from the car, coming around to help her out. She placed her hands on his shoulders and slid down, Ryan making sure there was a reasonable distance between their bodies. 'You're far too tempting, Beth Durant.' Although the words were harsh, there was a look of wonderment in his eyes and one of those small smiles she loved, caressing his lips.

'Likewise,' she retorted.

His smile grew. 'You know we're going to be the talk of the hospital?'

Beth shrugged. 'I have more important things to focus on than hospital gossip.'

'Yes, you do.' He checked his watch as they took their bags from the car. 'You have about ten minutes before ward round. Go check on your parents.'

They started walking towards the hospital. 'Are you in Theatre with me this morning?'

'I have a meeting scheduled for nine, but I'll try and get there after that.'

'OK.' She paused, then said, 'Ryan.' Beth swallowed, feeling a little nervous about what she was going to say but knowing she needed to say it. 'Would you…mind coming with me to see my parents?'

His look was one of genuine concern as they entered the hospital and headed towards the orthopaedic department. 'You all right?'

'Well, Phil is going to tell us the results this morning and if it's that Dad needs to be in a wheelchair, well…although I've been preparing myself to hear those words, I still don't know if I can deal with them.'

'Of course.' He took her free hand in his and gave it a little squeeze. 'Just let me check in with my secretaries and then I'll meet you there.'

'Are you sure? Because if you'd rather not, I—'

He stopped walking, pulling her to a halt. 'Thank you for asking me.'

'Oh. Good. OK. It's just I didn't want you to think it was one of my crazy tests because it isn't. Honestly. I just need someone to…be there. I have to be strong for both my parents and I don't know how my mother is going to react and—'

Ryan bent his head and pressed a kiss to her lips, silencing her. It did the trick. Right there, in the middle of a hospital corridor, Ryan kissed her.

He pulled back. 'It's no trouble. I'll see you there.' With that he turned and headed towards his office block.

Beth stood there for a moment, stunned. That, she hadn't expected. It took more than a moment to get herself under control once more and she shook her head, delighted with his willing openness. He never ceased to surprise her and that, she realized was one of the things she loved so much about him.

With a smile on her face and a spring in her step, she headed to see her father, anxious to hear the latest information on his condition.

'Good morning, darling,' Isabelle greeted her. 'You're looking quite chipper.'

Beth kissed her mother. 'Feeling it.'

'It's Ryan, isn't it,' her mother stated.

'Ryan?' her father asked, a little confused.

'Remember I was telling you? You know, the man Beth's house-sitting with.'

Daniel looked at his daughter after she'd kissed his cheek. 'Should I be grilling him?'

'No.' Beth smiled at her father. 'You should be concentrating on getting better.' She asked them both how they'd slept, glad to hear her mother had slept quite well in the residential wing.

'I'll organise a hotel later today, once we know what the status is with your father.'

'I can arrange for you to stay in the residential wing for a few more nights. It'll make life a bit easier for you.'

'That would be lovely, dear.'

Beth read her father's chart, glad to see he'd managed to sleep without too much pain. A few minutes later Ryan walked into the ward and crossed to Beth's side.

'Good morning.' He smiled at her mother and then looked down at her father. 'How are you feeling this morning, Dan-el?' He took the chart from Beth and scanned it with obvious satisfaction.

'I've been better.'

'Ryan. It's so good to see you again,' Isabelle crooned.

'This is Ryan?' Daniel was confused. 'Have we met before?'

Ryan smiled. 'A few times, but it's quite normal that you don't remember.'

'So you're the man I should be grilling,' Daniel said gruffly.

'Dad!' Beth groaned.

'What, pet? It's a father's right to grill the man who's inter-ested in his daughter.'

Beth glanced at Ryan, wondering what to do. He was smil-ing down at her father. 'I look forward to it.'

'Smooth talker.' Isabelle giggled.

'Everyone's here,' Phil said as he walked towards Daniel's bed. 'Ready for Theatre, Daniel?'

'Ready as I'll ever be.'

'What's the verdict, Phil?' Beth asked the question which she knew her parents were too anxious to ask out loud.

'We'll be doing the CT myelogram to give a better delinea-ion of the bony anatomy and the specific nerve roots' involve-ment. However, things are still looking hopeful.'

Beth shifted closer to Ryan and grabbed his hand, holding it tight.

'So today, once we've done the myelogram, I'll be perform-ing a laminectomy and posterior foraminotomy at the involved levels.'

'Meaning?' Isabelle asked.

'Meaning things are looking good.'

Tears began to fill Isabelle's eyes. 'He won't need to be in a wheelchair?'

'Not this time.'

'Oh. Oh.' Isabelle began to shake and Beth quickly let go of Ryan's hand and rushed to her mother's side.

'It's all right, Mum. Let it go.'

'He's going to be all right,' Isabelle said through a wash of tears.

'There she goes,' Daniel said. 'Now that the fuss is over, she can fall apart.'

Beth held her mother close as Isabelle wept onto her shoulder. 'He's going to be all right,' she kept saying.

'Phil will take care of him. Phil always does,' Beth said softly.

Ryan's pager beeped and so did Beth's. 'Ward round calls,' Ryan said.

Isabelle wiped at her eyes with a handkerchief. 'Off you go, Beth. Go and see to your patients.'

'You'll be all right?'

'Hey? What about me?' Daniel complained, and Beth kissed his cheek again.

'You're already getting all the attention.'

'True and, boy, oh, boy, do I like it.'

Beth turned to Phil. 'What time will you start Theatre?'

'Half past nine, in theatre three.'

'I'll be in theatre one this morning,' Beth told him.

Phil nodded. 'I'll make sure you're kept informed.'

'Thanks.'

Ryan waited for Beth and the two of them headed down to the orthopaedic ward. 'Is your mum going to be OK?'

Beth smiled. 'Yes. She'll cry for most of today and tomorrow and when dad's improving, she'll bounce back to her normal self again.'

'You should really be with her while your dad's in Theatre.'

'Nothing I can do about that. I have my own theatre list to contend with, but the staff will look after her. Tristan will probably drop by and several of the staff from the spinal ward know my parents well. She'll be fine.'

'I can get out of my meeting and take over the theatre list.'

'It's all right. I'd go crazy just sitting there, waiting for information. No. I'd rather keep busy in Theatre.'

'You'll be able to concentrate?'

She frowned. 'Concerned?'

'I just need to make sure you're up to it.'

'I'll be fine. Phil will keep me informed, like he said, and that'll help.'

'All right, then, but promise to tell me if you're not right with things?'

Her frown increased. 'You don't trust me to do my job? Is that it?'

'No, that's not it. I'm not picking on you, Beth, I just need to ensure the best possible outcome for all concerned. I can't have you thinking about your father when you're in the middle of a hip replacement.'

'I resent that.'

'I thought you might. Look, there are extenuating circumstances. It's not every day your father has surgery and you're permitted to take time out to simply be his daughter rather than being an orthopaedic registrar.'

Beth shook her head as they entered the ward. 'I knew Sir Ryan would raise his ugly head today.'

'That's not what this is about.'

Her pager sounded and she checked the number, noting it was emergency Theatres. 'I'll be fine,' she told him, and headed off to the nurses' station to answer her page. 'Dr Durant. Someone paged me?'

'Yes,' Theatre Sister said. 'Tristan wants a word with you.'

A moment later, Tristan's voice came down the line. 'Beth. I won't make ward round. That girl you scraped off the road the other night has developed complications. She's being anaesthetised right now and I need your help. I know the elective list starts at nine but if you could give me the next forty-five minutes or so, that would be great.'

'I'm on my way,' she said, glad to get out of the ward round and therefore having to deal with Ryan's behaviour. She headed over to where Ryan was talking to a very pretty intern. The intern was smiling up at him with stars in her eyes, and a thread of annoyance coursed through Beth. She glanced at Ryan to see him with his Sir Ryan mask on, ignoring all pheromones coming his way, and felt her annoyance wane.

'Excuse me, Sir Ryan,' Beth said, and was a little surprised when Ryan turned quickly to face her.

'Ah, Dr Durant. Good. Excuse me,' he said to the intern, and placed his hand beneath Beth's elbow and propelled her over to a corner. 'You have that information for me?' he said loudly enough for the intern to hear.

'What are you talking about?' Beth asked, completely confused.

'Just go with me on this. If the woman had batted her eyelashes at me one more time, I might have laughed out loud.'

Beth couldn't help the smile that came to her lips. 'Tut-tut. You must be professional, Sir Ryan, at *all* times.'

'Cut it out. What's up?'

'Tristan needs me in Emergency Theatres. The girl who was hit on Saturday night has developed complications.'

'Has she regained consciousness yet?'

'Yes. Her name's Denise and her family have been notified so at least she's no longer all alone.'

'Right. You go. I'll cancel my meeting and meet you in emergency Theatres. After that, you can head up to elective Theatres and start there. Once Tristan and I are done, we'll take over the elective list and you can be there when your dad comes out of the anaesthetic.'

'You're organising again.'

'That's my job.'

Beth sighed and nodded. It was true. Although she needed to keep busy while her father was under the knife, she would also like to be there when he came out of Theatre. 'All right. You go and enjoy ward round with your little intern friend and I'll see you soon.'

He smiled, his professional mask in place. 'You'll pay later for that comment.'

'Ooh. I can hardly wait.' Beth headed out of the ward, glancing over her shoulder to see him standing there, watching her walk away. She giggled and then sighed again, amazed at how she could feel exasperated and happy with him at the same time.

She wasn't used to being told what to do, especially where

her private life was concerned. Was that something she would have to get used to if she let Ryan into her inner sanctum? He was already there in spirit because she was so in love with him, but physically? She realised the idea of loving Ryan and the physical reality of it were definitely going to bring problems.

She changed and scrubbed before heading into Theatre.

'And about time, too,' Tristan grumbled. 'What have you been doing? Standing around, making moon eyes at our new boss?'

Beth glanced at the staff in the room and realised they were all looking at her expectantly, waiting for her answer. Had they heard the gossip already? The fact that Tristan was openly joking about it was her clue that she and Ryan had already been discussed.

'Or were you just smooching in the corridor, as has already been reported this morning?' Tristan continued, and winked at her.

Beth smiled beneath her mask. 'Is there a box for "all of the above"?'

One of the sisters gasped. 'Really? You're together?'

'Looks that way,' Beth answered. 'Ryan said he'd come and take over from me so I can start the elective list on time, so we'd better get started. What's the situation?'

'Well,' Tristan said, looking down at the patient, 'Denise decided she wanted to go a few more rounds on the operating table and has presented us with an interesting challenge. Compartment syndrome in the right arm, swelling around the top of the femur, and it looks as though her left third metacarpal will need microsurgery if we're going to save it.'

'Just as well Ryan's coming, then.'

'Kind of nice to have someone with his expertise in microsurgery on staff,' Tristan murmured. 'Right. Let's fix this compartment syndrome before we go any further.'

Ryan arrived sooner than they'd anticipated and was able to take a good look at Denise's finger, reviewing the scans that had already been taken.

'How does it look?' Beth asked while they waited for check radiographs to be taken.

'I've seen worse.'

'I'll bet you have.' She glanced up at the clock and Ryan followed her gaze.

'You'd better get up to elective Theatres. I may only be new to this hospital but a late starting theatre list is time and money our department can't stand to lose—in fact, it's that way in most hospitals around the globe.'

'Except for those out in the jungle, eh? OK. I'll leave you boys to play heroes.'

As she headed out, Ryan stopped her and said softly, 'Go check on your parents before you head in. Being a few minutes late shouldn't matter.'

She met his gaze and nodded. 'Thanks.'

'Will you two quit it?' Tristan grumbled. 'With all the *lurv* you're both exhibiting, you're making me want to rush home to my wife!'

Beth held her breath for a moment, wondering if Tristan had overstepped the mark. She glanced at Ryan, then at Tristan and back at Ryan. She could tell he was smiling beneath his mask as his blue eyes were twinkling.

'First thing's first, Casanova. Let's get Denise organised.'

Tristan laughed. 'Right you are. Away with you, Beth, and give my regards to your parents.'

Beth nodded and headed out. As she degowned and headed up to elective Theatres, she tried not to dwell on her father's operation. Ryan was right. She had to focus, she had to be professional, but it was difficult when your father was having major surgery in the theatre a few doors down. Still, she'd told him she could handle it and handle it she would. She wasn't going to let down the man she loved.

She headed straight for theatre three's pre-med area. Her mother was sitting on a stool beside her father's bed, holding his hand. 'How is he?' Beth asked as she put her arm around Isabelle's shoulders.

'Away with the fairies,' Daniel muttered. 'And having quite a lovely time of it.'

Beth smiled. Just like her dad to keep his sense of humour even after a pre-med. The anaesthetist came up and spoke to them, saying he'd be taking Daniel through to Theatre now. Both Beth and her mother kissed him.

'He's not so bad,' Daniel said, his voice croaky.

'Who?' Beth asked.

'That fellow of yours. Ryan.'

Beth kissed his cheek again. 'Stay safe. I love you, Dad.'

'Love you, too, my Beth.'

As he was wheeled away, Beth held her mother's hand then took her to the doctors' tearoom. 'I'm sorry I can't wait with you, Mum.'

'Don't apologise, Beth. Your dad and I understand your job.'

'Will you be all right?' She handed her mother a cup of tea.

'Yes. I have a few things I need to get done so don't you worry about me. Tristan's in Theatre, isn't he?'

'Yes, and I'm not sure how long he'll be.' Her pager started beeping and she knew she had to leave.

'Go, dear. Phil will keep us informed. He always does.'

Beth smiled. 'If you need anything—and I mean *anything*— you just let the staff know you're my mother, and if they don't jump to it, there'll be trouble.'

Isabelle laughed. 'Even your Ryan?'

'Mum,' Beth groaned, and Isabelle's tinkling laughter filled the room once more, helping to lighten the load on Beth's heart.

'Go, dear.'

Beth kissed her mother and went to see her first patient. As she scrubbed, she compartmentalised her emotions and thoughts so that when she entered Theatre, she was Dr Beth Durant, orthopaedic registrar, ready to get to work.

She was halfway through her third arthroscopy when Ryan walked in.

'How's Denise?'

'Holding her own.'

'And her finger?'

'Looking a lot better than before. Still.' He shrugged. 'It's too early to call.' He glanced at the phone in the corner. 'Any news about your dad?'

'Phil called about an hour ago to say he'd done the myelogram and the results were just what he needed so he's hoping for minimal complications, if any.'

'That's good news.'

'I thought so.'

'What have you got left on this list?'

'Two partial lateral meniscectomies.'

'Good. They shouldn't take too long. Clinic might actually start on time this afternoon.'

'More saved money for the department?' She smiled at him knowing he would hear the teasing note in her voice.

'Jest all you like, but as head of department, it's my job to crunch numbers and make sure things are adding up.'

'One of your jobs.'

'Yes, and I've got to go to Melbourne on Wednesday for—'

The instrument Beth had been holding slipped from her hand and clattered to the floor, startling not only herself but a few of the staff as well. 'Er…sorry.' She waited for a clean replacement to be placed into her waiting palm. 'Melbourne on Wednesday?' She'd forgotten he would be travelling. She wondered how long he'd be away.

'Only until Saturday,' he continued, answering her unspoken question. 'Training staff around the country was also part of my contract.'

'Surely they could have given you longer than a week to settle in.'

'Apparently not.'

The phone rang and the scout nurse answered. 'It's Phil,' she told Beth.

'Here, give me that.' Ryan took the instrument she'd just put down. 'Go see what he has to say.'

Beth headed over to the phone and the scout nurse held the receiver to her ear. 'Phil?'

'Things are looking good, Beth. I'm almost done and the damage wasn't nearly as bad as I'd anticipated.'

Beth sighed with the utmost relief. 'Thank you, Phil.'

'He'll be out in another hour.'

'Excellent.' She nodded for the nurse to remove the phone but didn't move for a few seconds.

'Good news?' Ryan asked.

She repeated what Phil had said and Ryan nodded. 'That is excellent. Why don't you head out and I'll finish up here?'

'No. It's all right. He'll be another hour.'

'Go. See your mother.'

'I'm all right, Ryan,' she insisted.

'Is she always this stubborn?' he asked Theatre Sister.

'Absolutely, Sir Ryan.'

'Terrific. Just what I need.' There was humour behind his words as Beth rejoined him at the operating table, but once the surgery was finished, Ryan came up and placed a hand on her shoulder. 'Go, Beth. I can see it in your eyes and I don't want you burning out. This is a highly emotional time for you and your mother. Go and see her now, then you can make it to clinic.'

'So that's your motive. Get my personal life sorted out so I can make it to clinic?' She tried to joke but it fell flat as she realised he was right. 'How do you know me so well?'

He shrugged and bent to kiss her forehead. 'Stop trying to be strong on your own. Lean on me, Beth, and let me help you.'

She looked up at him. 'It's been so long since I've leaned on anyone, Ryan, I'm not sure I can do it.'

'Trust me,' he said. 'I'm not Jeff and I'm not as shallow as those other men you dated.'

'I know,' she whispered, tears filling her eyes as wave after wave of emotion started to crash over her. Ryan gathered her into his arms and simply held her as she sobbed. The pressure she'd been trying to control ever since she'd learned of her father's ill-health now broke down and came flooding out. At first she was a little self-conscious that Ryan was the one who should witness her like this, but as he tightened his arms around her, she realised he was the perfect person.

When she'd finished, he handed her a tissue and after she'd blown her nose, he pressed a quick kiss to her lips. 'I'll see you in clinic.'

She nodded and sniffed. 'OK.'

'Give Isabelle my regards.'

'If I can find her,' Beth said.

'She'll be around, close by.'

'Yes.' Beth smiled at him. 'Thanks.'

'That's what I'm here for.' His smile gave her the strength to head out and go in search of her mother. She wasn't in the doctors' tearoom, not that Beth had expected Isabelle to stay put. She was a people person and right now she'd need to be surrounded by people. Beth headed back to emergency Theatres and changed back into her suit, feeling more in control of her emotions.

She checked on Denise, pleased the woman was stable, and then headed to the spinal ward. 'She's gone to Paediatrics,' the ward sister told her. 'Said it would help. I've already promised to relay any calls down there so feel free to wander down.'

Of course. The paediatric ward would be the perfect place for her mother to spend time, and Beth headed there immediately. As she walked in, she was greeted with a curt nod by Sister Dorset, who ran the ward. Beth smiled back at the other woman, knowing that beneath her brisk, no-nonsense exterior there was a heart of gold.

'Your mother is in the games room, doing craft with some of the children,' Sister Dorset informed her. 'I trust your father's operation is proceeding well?'

'Yes, Sister.' Beth looked around the ward. It felt different without Marty and Natalie there, but that was to be expected.

'Very good. Your mother is more than welcome to stay for as long as she likes, Doctor, but if you wouldn't mind removing the larrikin who came with her, I would appreciate it. He razzes up the children almost as much as Dr Williams.'

Beth listened and heard Tristan's laugh. 'I don't think anyone could razz the children up the way Marty does,' she agreed. 'Although it sounds like Tristan's giving it a pretty good shot.'

Beth headed to the games room and passed on Sister's message. Tristan quickly reverted to his meek and mild persona. They stayed there for the next three quarters of an hour and when

the call came to say Daniel was out of Theatre and being taken
to Recovery, Beth and Isabelle said goodbye to the children.

'You'd better come, too, Tris,' Beth said. 'Or else Sister Dorset
will have a fruity.'

'What's a fruity?' one of the children asked with an inno-
cent smile.

'It means she may get cross with me for making too much
noise,' Tristan explained as he, too, said goodbye. They all
headed up to Recovery and Beth was surprised to find Ryan
standing at the end of her father's bed, chatting softly with Phil.

He cared. He *really* cared.

Beth stopped in the doorway and stared at him, her heart
melting. All she wanted was to rush up to him and find security,
happiness and love in his arms. It was the strangest sensation and
one she'd never felt before. She knew he was important to her
life but she'd only hoped to one day find a man who would make
her feel the way Ryan was making her feel now…just through
his natural ability to care for those people she loved the most.

He'd ploughed through her check-list, knocking it on its head,
and now he'd passed one more test. He really cared. It was as
though the check-list, the silly little check-list she'd created simply to protect herself, was insignificant. She loved Ryan and
he'd asked her to trust him. She'd already taken the first step
when she'd cried in front of him, and that had given her courage
to climb another rung on the trust ladder.

Ryan turned and looked over at her, standing stock-still in the
doorway. Isabelle and Tristan had continued into the room but
Beth had found herself rooted to the spot. Ryan held her gaze
and walked silently towards her. He didn't say anything, just
stood in front of her, looking down into her upturned face. For
a moment neither of them spoke and for that moment Beth felt
they were connected by a strong invisible barrier that would
bind them together for all time. It felt as though the rest of the
world had disappeared and there was only the two of them, their
hearts beating as one.

Slowly and with a tenderness she drank in, Ryan reached out

and took her hand in his, giving it a reassuring squeeze. Again, as there didn't seem to be the need for words, he silently led her towards her father's bed. Feeling secure, with Ryan's hand holding hers, Beth looked down at her father and more of the anguish and uncertainty she'd worked hard at repressing began to flow forth.

Tears pricked behind her eyes as she bent down to kiss his forehead. She sniffed for a moment before turning to Phil. 'Everything…?' The words stuck in her throat and she quickly cleared it.

'Everything went better than expected,' Phil reported, and held out the chart to her. It was then that Ryan let go of Beth's hand, but once she'd scanned the notes and handed them back to Phil, she felt the warmth of his fingers return to hers.

Tristan's pager sounded and he quickly excused himself, heading out of Recovery. Beth and Ryan stayed a few more minutes before heading out. 'I'll be in clinic so you call me if you need anything,' Beth told her mother before leaving. Isabelle merely nodded, her grip almost fierce on her husband's hand.

'You all right to do clinic?' Ryan asked as they headed down the corridor, their hands still entwined.

Beth breathed in deeply and let out a big sigh. 'Yes. He's out, he's better. I'm good now.' She cleared her throat again. 'Oh, and thanks for before.'

'Before?'

'My breakdown.'

Ryan smiled at her. 'I'm surprised you held out that long.'

'Well…thanks.'

'My pleasure.' He gave her hand one last squeeze as they headed into Outpatients. Clinic flowed smoothly without too many complications, and when it was over Beth headed to the high-dependency unit to check on her father. Ryan had gone to see his secretaries and pick up some paperwork.

'Where's Ryan?' Isabelle asked as Beth walked in.

'He's not glued to my side, Mum.'

'He was earlier. So nice of him to be so supportive.'

'Mmm. How's Dad?' Beth read his nursing chart, happy with his progress.

'He's slowly getting more colour back into his face. It's going to be another long haul but—'

'But not as long as we'd initially thought,' Beth finished. 'Listen. It's getting late. Why don't we both have dinner, then you can go and rest while I take the night vigil?'

'You don't have to.'

'I want to.'

'I know, dear, but you have work tomorrow and—'

'I'll be fine. I've stayed here many a night. What's one more?'

When Ryan came to see her, his briefcase in his hand, she told him of her plans. He nodded and took her aside so they could talk more privately. 'Why don't I take you and your mother out to dinner, then you can go home, grab a change of clothes and I'll bring you back to the hospital?'

'You don't have to—'

He leaned in and placed a finger over her lips. 'I want to.'

Beth felt her heart rate increase, her breathing become shallow and her knees turn to jelly at the touch. Why did this man have the power to affect her so completely *and* with just one small intimate gesture?

She looked up into his eyes but realised there was more going on here than he was telling her. 'What is it?' she asked.

Ryan stepped away and raked a hand through his hair, exhaling in exasperation. 'It's uncanny that you know when something's wrong.'

'Tell me about it. This…connection we have is getting stronger.'

Ryan nodded and paused before saying, 'My flight to Melbourne leaves tomorrow.'

'Tomorrow? I thought you weren't going until Wednesday?'

'So did I. There have been some changes in Melbourne and I start at ten o'clock tomorrow morning. My secretaries have spent most of the day reorganising my schedule.' Ryan put his hand on her shoulder. 'So let's go out to dinner and celebrate the success of Daniel's operation.' His thumb was rubbing gently in a circular motion, causing little tingles to spread down her arm before they burst throughout the rest of her.

'OK.' She smiled up at him. 'That's what we'll do.' She wanted to jump up and down, to rant and scream, to demand that he didn't go, but she knew that was as irrational as she felt. Instead, she went and told her mother of the change in plans. Isabelle physically preened and looked up at Ryan with delight.

'What an excellent idea, Ryan. I'm more than ready to go now.' She stood, then faltered for a second. 'The hospital will call if there's any change, won't they?'

'Absolutely,' Beth and Ryan said in unison, then smiled at each other. 'Come on, Mum. Let's go before Ryan changes his mind and we end up in the hospital cafeteria which, incidentally, was where I was planning to take you.'

Isabelle's tinkling laugh filled the area and after they'd told the sister of their plans, Ryan escorted the two Durant women from the hospital. They had a wonderful dinner and afterwards Ryan took them back to Marty's house for Beth to pack her bag. Isabelle wandered around the house, oohing and ahhing and saying how Natalie would be so happy living there.

When Beth was ready, she took her bag to the door and was surprised to see Ryan walking towards her, a bag slung over his shoulder. 'What are you doing?'

'Packing for my trip to Melbourne.'

'But your plane doesn't leave until six o'clock in the morning.'

'I know. I thought I might hang around the hospital tonight and leave from there in the morning.' He shrugged. 'It's closer to the airport and that way, you can use Marty's car and I'll order a taxi to take me to the airport.' He put his bag on the floor and gathered her into his arms. 'Also,' he said softly, 'I find that at the moment I can't stay away from you. Sappy, I know, but that's the way it is.'

She smiled up at him and he brushed a quick kiss across her lips. 'I know the feeling.'

They took Isabelle to the residential wing and then Beth returned to the ward to sit by her father's bed. Ryan went to his office and managed to get through his mound of paperwork, appearing every few hours with a fresh cup of coffee to revitalse Beth. Daniel remained stable throughout the night and just before five a.m. Isabelle appeared.

'Mum.' Beth sat up straighter in the chair and yawned. 'What are you doing here? Go back to bed.'

'You go and get showered and changed, then go with Ryan to the airport. The two of you deserve at least half an hour away from this place and everyone in it, even if that's just a drive to the airport.'

Beth nodded and did as she was told, turning up in Ryan's office just as he was packing things away.

'You look like a breath of fresh air.' He smiled as she walked over to his side. 'How's Daniel?'

'Sleeping peacefully.'

'Excellent.'

'I'm coming to the airport with you.'

Ryan nodded, his gaze never leaving hers. 'Then we'd better get going. Your mother insisted I call Arnold, and I presume he's downstairs, waiting.'

'OK.'

'Beth.' Ryan stood from his chair, desire raging in his gaze as he drew her close, his mouth meeting hers with an urgency that didn't surprise either of them in the slightest. After a while he pulled back, both of them breathless. 'We need to go.'

'I know.'

Arnold was waiting outside the front of the hospital and greeted them both warmly. 'You two sit back and relax. I'll get you there safely, Dr Cooper.'

They sat in the back and held hands, occasionally kissing or just gazing into each other's eyes. After a while Ryan said softly, 'Today has been a revelation.'

'Hmm?' Beth looked up at him from beneath her lashes.

'Letting myself touch you, being allowed to kiss you, to offer comfort and support. It's quite, quite amazing, Beth.'

She nodded. 'I know. I feel the same.'

'When I get back, we'll need to talk.'

She nodded again. 'When are you back?'

'Saturday, but I'm away again on Monday, or Sunday night, or something ridiculous like that.'

Beth leaned her head against his arm. 'I'll miss you.'

When they arrived at the airport, Ryan handed over Marty's car keys and took her in his arms, kissing her tenderly. They'd arrived late and he'd been rushed through check-in and now the time had come for them to part, and it was the last thing either of them wanted to do.

'I'm fairly certain I'm in love with you, Beth.'

At the words, her world began to spin. She gulped over the sudden dryness in her throat.

'I'm in love with you, too,' she whispered, gazing up at him with delight.

Again he kissed her but they were interrupted by the flight attendant telling him the flight was boarding and he needed to get on immediately.

'I don't know if I'll get time to call,' he said. 'My schedule is very hectic, but I'll be thinking of you.' He pressed his lips to hers once more…and then he was gone, leaving her body tingling and her heart singing at their new discovery. Ryan loved her!

CHAPTER TWELVE

BETH convinced her mother to move into the house with her as there was still one unoccupied bedroom.

'Your house is rented out, and with Dad in the hospital your only other option is a hotel, and that's just ridiculous when there's room at Nat and Marty's.'

'Do you think Marty would mind?'

'I think he'd be cross if you didn't accept. He has a strong sense of family, just like Ryan.'

'Speaking of Ryan, how was your trip to the airport?'

Beth thought for a moment, wondering about the best way to answer. Although she and Ryan had said they loved each other, there was still much to be discussed. Her emotions were so new, so overwhelming that she wasn't ready to share them just yet and, besides, her mother had enough to concentrate on for now. 'Peaceful, relaxing,' she finally said.

'Good.'

Isabelle moved into Marty's house that evening and Beth was glad of the company. There was no word from Ryan for the next few days and Beth forced herself to focus on work, spending time with her father or watching a movie with her mother in the evenings when she wasn't at the hospital. All the time she carried with her that secret spark of love…along with a lot of doubts.

Was she really in love or just infatuated? Did love to Ryan

mean the same as it did to her? Was he getting through his work-load? Was he getting enough sleep? Was he missing her?

On Friday evening, just as she was getting into bed, her cell-phone rang and she picked it up, positive it was the hospital. Denise was getting better slowly, but Beth and Tristan had taken her back to Theatre yet again that afternoon to further debride her wound. 'Dr Durant,' she said into the receiver.

'Ah…Beth, my love. The sound of your voice is like music to my ears.'

'Ryan!'

'You were expecting your other boyfriend?'

Boyfriend! Beth smiled at the word. She hadn't really thought that far but she guessed that's exactly what he was…at the moment. 'No. I was expecting the hospital.' She quickly explained about Denise.

'Yes, I heard.'

'Heard what?'

'That you'd taken Denise back to Theatre.'

Beth frowned. 'How did you—?'

'My secretary told me.'

'Oh.' He'd had time to call his secretary but not her? Beth pushed the thought aside. His secretaries were paid to be at work at all hours, doing his bidding. 'But let's not talk about work. How are you? Everything going smoothly?'

'There have been a few hiccups.'

'Does this mean your trip will be extended?'

'No.' The word was direct and emphatic. 'I'll be back in Sydney by tomorrow afternoon.'

'I'm on call.'

'I'll try and catch up with you at the hospital, then.'

'You could always join me in Theatre.'

'Ugh,' he groaned. 'I've had enough of operating and teach-ing and everything. I've just spoken to my secretary and I have a meeting at the hospital tomorrow afternoon about half an hour after I get back.'

'On a Saturday?'

'It was the only time the heads of units could get together. Everyone's been hectic and I fly out again on Sunday evening.'

Beth felt her spirits plummet but she forced her voice to sound bright and cheery as she snuggled beneath the covers. 'Where to next?'

'Perth.'

She sighed. 'So…have you had time to catch up with some of your old work colleagues?'

'I've been unable to avoid it. I've taught at six different hospitals so far and each one has had either a lunch or dinner in my honour.'

'Sounds like fun.'

'It isn't…at least, without you it isn't.'

Beth felt all warm and fuzzy at his words. 'So where are you now?'

'Hotel. I've just got in. As the guest of honour, it's hard to leave early.'

Beth smiled. 'I remember.'

'Of course. Our Christmas dinner, where we first met. That was an…interesting night.'

'Meaning?'

'Meaning you looked amazing in that dress.'

'I felt overdressed.'

'No. No. You were perfect. I wanted to ask you to join me after the dinner for a drink, but we were interrupted.'

'Hmm. I remember, and then you became narky.'

'You were paying too much attention to Tristan.'

Beth's eyes widened. 'You were jealous?'

'Surprised?'

'Yes.'

'You were the most beautiful woman I'd seen in a long time and I wanted to leave that restaurant with you the instant you walked in the door.'

'How did you know who I was? I could have been another patron not associated with the hospital.'

'Marty had described you.'

'He did what?'

Ryan chuckled. 'He also told me you were special—and you know something? He was right.'

Beth breathed in deeply and sighed, warmed by the words he was saying.

'It's late and you're probably going to be woken in a few hours with a call to Theatre so I'll let you get to bed.'

'I'm already there.'

Silence. 'You're all snuggled in bed?'

'Yes.'

'Hair loose?' His voice became thick with desire.

'Yes.'

'What are you wearing? No,' he added quickly. 'On second thoughts, don't tell me. I have meetings in the morning, then the flight back to Sydney and more meetings. I need to sleep, too.'

Beth chuckled. 'Flannelette pyjamas, Ryan. They're hardly sexy.'

'Hey, you look amazing in theatre scrubs, Beth.'

'Get some sleep.'

'I'll be there tomorrow night and I want to see you in the pyjamas because I seriously don't believe that you don't look sexy in them.'

'My mother's staying here,' she blurted out. 'It seemed logical,' she continued in a rush.

'Probably just as well. Looks as though the pj inspection will have to wait.'

'You're nuts.'

'About you.'

'I love you,' she whispered.

'I love you, too,' he responded. 'Dream of me.'

Being the doctor on call, Beth was called to the hospital very early next morning to operate on patients from a bad motor vehicle accident. As the day progressed, she found herself clock-watching, something she rarely did. Had Ryan boarded the plane all right? Had he arrived in Sydney? Was he in the hospital? In his meeting?

When she finally finished in Theatre, she went to check on her father, who was making excellent progress.

'Where's Mum?'

'In the cafeteria, having something to eat. Hey, it's good to have Ryan back,' Daniel said, and Beth's eyes widened.

'You've seen him?'

'You haven't?' Daniel was surprised. 'Of course.' He pointed to her clothes. She was still dressed in theatre scrubs. 'You've been in Theatre. Yes, he left only a few minutes ago.'

Beth sighed and slumped into the chair beside her father's bed.

'Why don't you go and track him down?'

'He'll be busy. He had meetings and paperwork and all sorts of things to deal with. I'll catch up with him some time, I guess.' A few minutes later her pager beeped and she groaned when she saw who needed her. 'A and E. I've got to go, Dad.' She kissed his cheek and headed to A and E, her gaze scouring every corridor she passed in case Ryan was standing there…but he wasn't.

'Beth, we have an ambulance due in with a teenage girl, Simone Atkins, who came off the back of a motorbike. Her leg's been partially amputated and the paramedics say she's losing ground fast.'

'Right. Prep emergency theatre one, have the radiographer standing by, and when she comes in, get her cross-typed and matched. Two units of plasma, three units of blood. Any allergies?'

'None reported.'

'Find Sir Ryan. This is his area of expertise.'

'He's back?'

'He's in the hospital. Call one of his secretaries. They always know where he is.' She tried to keep the annoyance out of her tone but wasn't sure she succeeded. 'What's the ETA on the ambulance?'

Triage Sister checked her watch. 'Two minutes.'

'Right. I'll go get scrubbed. Bring her straight through. Joey's the anaesthetist. Where is he?'

'He should be here. I'll sort him out. You go get ready.'

'Thanks.'

Beth had been in Theatre with Simone for fifteen minutes before she felt rather than saw Ryan walk in. She glanced up, her gaze meeting his. They seemed to devour each other for a moment before Beth cleared her throat and said, 'Thanks for coming.'

'What have we got?' he asked, walking over to the X-rays, which were up on the viewer.

'At the moment I'm trying to control the bleeding.'

He walked back to the operating table, standing opposite her. 'Once she's stabilised, I'd like 3-D scans of the leg.'

'I'll get that organised, Sir Ryan,' Theatre Sister said, and nodded to the scout nurse.

'Looks as though I get my own private lesson in your technique,' Beth said evenly.

'I guess you do.' Ryan was definitely all business but, then, so was Beth. She was in awe of Ryan's skill, realising not for the first time what a brilliant surgeon he really was. Once the circulation supply had been re-established and Simone was in a more stable condition, she was taken to Radiography for the three-dimensional scans Ryan required. The operation couldn't proceed without them. Glad of the short break, Beth degowned and rubbed at her eyes.

Warm hands landed on her shoulders and began massaging. 'Mmm.'

'Nice?' His deep voice washed over her, causing goose-bumps to ripple down her arms.

'Mmm.'

'This wasn't quite the reunion I'd planned.'

'Me either.'

He turned her to face him and wrapped his arms around her, bringing his mouth to meet hers in one swift motion. This was what both of them needed, to feel the brand-new love that flowed between them. 'I've missed you.'

'I'd hoped you had.'

He raised his eyebrows. 'You didn't miss me?'

She smiled coyly. 'Haven't had time. You see, the new orthopaedic director has been out of town, which means more work for the rest of us.'

'Scoundrel.'

'Hmm.' She stood on tiptoe and kissed his lips.

'What was that for?'

'I missed you, too.'

Ryan smiled. 'I should hope so. I was planning to take you out this evening, but it looks as though we're going to be spending most of it in Theatre.'

She shrugged. 'Such is life. I do have some good news, though. Elise Cartwright's pelvic fracture looks as though it doesn't need surgery.'

'That is good news.'

Beth smiled at him. 'I'm just sorry you're stuck in a theatre once more.'

'Giving another lesson.'

'I know you're sick and tired of being in Theatre,' she said softly, wishing she could help him through his exhaustion and fatigue.

He nodded and smiled at her. 'Nothing we can do about it.' He let her go. 'Let's sit down and I'll go over the technique in detail.'

By the time they'd finished in Theatre it was well into the early hours of Sunday morning and when they arrived back at Marty's they were both exhausted.

'What's on your agenda?' she asked softly as they waited for the kettle to boil, both of them conscious of not wanting to wake Isabelle.

'Paperwork, meeting with a real estate agent to look over a house, seeing my parents and then preparing for Perth.'

'You're looking at a house?'

'Yes. My secretary found one within walking distance of the hospital, and from the way she described it, it's perfect.'

'Oh.' Beth couldn't believe what he was saying, although why it should come as a surprise she wasn't sure. She knew they couldn't stay on at Marty and Natalie's indefinitely. She'd been too wrapped up in her own little world, missing Ryan, worrying about her father, looking after her mother, to have done anything about finding somewhere to live. After all, she didn't have two secretaries doing her bidding.

'Here's your tea,' Ryan said, placing a cup in front of her.

'Thanks.' She listened as he spoke about his week, his flight and the meeting he'd had. She wondered whether he'd met up with Geraldine while he'd been in Melbourne but if he had, he wasn't mentioning it. She hoped that meant it wasn't important. When she couldn't successfully smother another yawn, Ryan smiled.

'Go to bed, Beth. You're exhausted.'

She nodded. 'I think I will.' She took her cup into the kitchen and put it in the dishwasher before letting Ryan pull her into his arms.

'You feel so good, honey.'

She rested her head against his chest, listening to his heart beating, trying desperately to get rid of the doubts that were growing by the minute. She'd thought all her doubts would vanish once she saw Ryan. Instead, she had more.

Beth wrapped her arms more tightly around him, knowing she had never before or ever would again feel this way about a man and still he was causing her angst. How could she love him and yet feel hurt by him at the same time? Didn't he realise she needed reassurance? And what about children? It was an issue they needed to sort out because she wanted children and she hoped he did, too, but would her genetic inheritance make him run in the other direction?

'Ryan? We need to talk.'

'Hmm?'

'About the future.' She felt him tense and closed her eyes momentarily. She needed to be strong, to have courage. '*Our* future.'

He shifted back slightly so he could look at her more easily. Beth wondered whether it was to put a bit of distance between them. 'What do you want to discuss?'

'You're withdrawing from me.'

'I'm just trying to look at you.'

'I'm not talking about physically but emotionally. Something's bothering you and I need you to tell me what that is.'

Ryan dropped his arms from around her and raked a hand through his hair. 'You're right.'

Beth gulped, feeling instantly cold. She didn't want to be right. She'd hoped he'd tell her it was just a figment of her imagination and that everything was perfect between them. Was he going to tell her that, although he loved her, he couldn't be with her long term? That she didn't fit his vision for his future? Her heart was pounding so wildly against her chest, if he didn't hurry up and speak, she was either going to hyperventilate or pass out.

'I just feel as though things are moving…a little too fast.'

'Too fast?'

He looked at her and saw the panic in her eyes. Gathering her back into his arms, he pressed a kiss to the top of her head. 'I still love you, Beth, but you have to try and understand that falling in love with you wasn't in my plan.'

'Wasn't scheduled in,' she said, trying desperately to lighten the moment.

'Exactly. I want to be with you but…' he shrugged '…I feel as though things are moving too fast. We've both been burned badly before and I need to slow things down. I want to enjoy our time together. We haven't really had a proper date yet.'

'Date,' she repeated, frowning.

'We need to get to know each other better. There are still so many things I don't know about you. Life's going to be hectic for a while, especially when I'm travelling the country, but if we can just slow things down, take our time, then we can really get to know each other better.'

Beth couldn't speak. Her mind was whirring frantically, trying to make sense of what he was saying. They stood there for a few more minutes before she realised she needed some space from him. As she faked another yawn, he picked up the cue.

'Definitely time for bed.' He eased back and she let go, knowing that holding onto him would do no good. He bent his head and kissed her in such a tender and loving way that for a moment she felt everything would work out between them. Reluctantly, they parted, Beth going through the mundane routine of getting changed for bed and brushing her teeth before the doubts returned once more.

In her world, saying the words 'I love you' to someone wasn't to be taken lightly. That meant it was a done deal. They would be together for ever and that was all there was to it but it appeared Ryan's definition of the words and hers were different.

His 'I love you' meant searching for a house and still doing his own thing. It meant spending more time at work than with her. It meant making time for everyone else in the world but the person he professed to love.

Tears began to roll down her cheeks. Her definition included security, marriage and, given their present lack-of-permanent-residence status, searching for a house *together*. He'd told her he wasn't looking for a relationship but she'd hoped, given the extent of their feelings for each other, that he'd changed his mind.

Obviously, she'd been wrong.

When Beth woke up after five hours' sleep, the thought of facing Ryan when her emotions were in complete turmoil was unbearable. She felt so…raw. Still, neither could she stay where she was. Flicking back the covers, she pulled on a tracksuit and her running shoes. She stuffed her phone and MP3 player in her pocket and opened her bedroom door.

It was just after six o'clock so she didn't expect her mother to be up yet, but the thought of running into Ryan had her heart beating wildly as she crept to the front door. Carefully, she opened it, glancing over her shoulder every few seconds to see if he was around. She wanted him to be and didn't at the same time. It was confusing.

'And that's why you need to get out,' she whispered to herself as she finally closed the door behind her. Taking off, she ran down the path and didn't stop running until she reached the jogging track. There she walked for a few minutes, trying desperately to make sense of her thoughts, but it was no use. She wanted the fairy-tale. Her parents had the fairy-tale. They'd met, they'd fallen in love, they'd got married, they were living their happily ever after. Why couldn't she get one?

Why did Ryan have to make everything so complicated? First she'd had to deal with his shift between Sir Ryan and the real Ryan, then she'd had to deal with her growing emotions towards the real Ryan and appreciating who Sir Ryan really was. Now, when they'd declared their feelings for each other, things still weren't black and white. She was putting herself out there. She was daring to trust, to take a chance, and she was petrified of getting hurt again. Jeff had said he'd loved her and then had run a mile. Ryan seemed to genuinely care for her parents, so if that wasn't the problem, what was? Didn't he trust her? He'd said he loved her but did he trust her? Was he brave enough to take that next step? She hoped so. Oh, she hoped so with all her heart. They'd both been hurt in the past but she knew the feelings of love she'd thought she'd felt for Jeff had been nothing compared to how she felt about Ryan. No, this time everything was more scary than before.

Turning up the volume on her music, she started to run again, concentrating on the songs instead of her thoughts. She knew how to compartmentalise; she had to do it every day at work so she could do it now.

It only lasted two songs before the words of the next song brought it all back. She gritted her teeth and tried the song after that but no matter which track she programmed, she found a way to connect it right back to Ryan and how he made her feel.

She stopped running and switched the music off, sitting down on a patch of grass, her knees up, her head in her hands. It wasn't fair. She had to talk to him. There was nothing else to do yet why should she have to? He'd said he loved her and in her mind the rest of their lives was as simple as that. She frowned, realising that love was never simple.

'You picked a great time to learn that lesson,' she mumbled as she stood up, feeling the dampness of the ground beneath her beginning to seep into her clothes. 'You need to talk to him again.' This time she said the words out loud, to make sure she took notice. 'Go and talk to him.'

By the time she arrived back at the house, it was close to seven o'clock. Letting herself in, she went into the kitchen to put the kettle on and found a note on the bench. She hoped it was better than the last note he'd left her.

Didn't want to wake you. At the hospital. Love, Ryan.

'Well, at least he remembers that he loves me,' Beth grumbled, and yanked open the fridge. 'Even if he doesn't act like it.'

'You mumbling again, dear?' Isabelle walked into the room and climbed onto a stool. 'Ooh, you look fit to be hog-tied.'

Beth smiled at her mother's reference. 'Too much time in America, Mum.' The smile slowly faded from her face as she recalled Ryan saying those words to her not that long ago. 'Tea?'

'Please. Where's Ryan?'

Beth gestured to the note she'd put back on the bench. 'Hospital.'

'Fair enough. I guess he's got quite a bit of work to catch up on, what with being away for most of the week.'

'Yeah. I guess.'

'You wanted him just to come home and spend time with you, didn't you, dear?'

'Oh Mum,' she wailed. 'I don't know what I expected, but it wasn't this.' She slumped down onto the bench and Isabelle put her hand on her daughter's head.

'Love isn't easy, dear.'

'So I'm discovering.'

'It's also hard when everything is so new and wonderful and exciting that he's not even around for you to enjoy it with. It's hard on him, too.'

She straightened. 'Is it? It doesn't seem to be.' Beth picked up the note. 'He didn't want to wake me.' She shook her head. 'He didn't even realise that I wasn't in the house!'

Isabelle frowned. 'How was he supposed to know that? Did you leave him a note?'

'No.'

'Then how? The man's not a mind-reader, Beth. He's just trying to navigate the waters of a new-found love while still doing his new-found job.'

'I know, but part of me doesn't want him to be sensible or rational. I want him to let go, to loosen up some more, to do something so completely out of the ordinary. Something wildly romantic that's going to make me swoon and that's going to blow his stuffy little mind.' The kettle boiled and switched itself off. 'Not literally, you understand.'

'I understand, dear.'

'Was Dad like this when you two first discovered you loved each other?'

Isabelle smiled. 'No. He knew what he wanted and he went after it, full steam ahead.'

'See?'

'But he also was working for himself and could take time out. Ryan has the hospital powers that be breathing down his neck, watching every step he takes. He has that knighthood weighing heavily around his neck, making people expect more from him than they have a right to. Added to that, he has to go around the country, teaching people how to do an operation. Throw you into the mix and he's got more than he can handle.'

'Are you saying I should just leave off, not pressure him and wait until the dust settles?'

'Can you do that?'

She frowned. 'I don't know.'

'Ha. I do. You can't. You're far too impatient, Beth. You've always known your own mind and when you decide on something, you stick to it without wavering. The problem with that excellent quality is that if your thoughts are allowed to run wild, you tend to shift your focus and run with the wrong thing—like your standard-dating. Oh, you find your way back onto the straight and narrow path in the end and, no doubt, you learn a lot of lessons by going off the path, but sometimes you need people…people who love you unconditionally to put you back on the path.'

'You think Ryan's the right path?'

'I do.'

'I need to talk to him.'

'Yes, but first let's have breakfast and get ready to go to the hospital. Your dad's going to be so pleased when he hears the news.' Isabelle clapped her hands happily.

'What news?'

'The news that you and Ryan have admitted your love for each other.' She paused. 'You have, haven't you?'

'Yes.' Beth turned and headed to her room to shower. 'And that seems to be where the trouble started.'

Ryan sat at his desk with his head in his hands, trying to figure out what he should do. He knew what he was supposed to be doing but instead of decreasing the amount of paperwork on his desk, he was thinking about Beth.

Business and pleasure didn't mix. He'd seen the results a thousand times and it ended up like oil and water. The tension of high-profile jobs, the long hours, the constant decision-making, playing with other people's lives. The stress inevitably took its toll and one person in the relationship had to take a back seat, career-wise, while the other surged ahead. Then feelings of inadequacy were raised and a whole new cycle began.

Then there were the emotions he was feeling. He loved Beth. With every fibre of his being he loved her, but he'd thought Geraldine had been the love of his life and he'd been wrong there. He knew Beth was nothing like Geraldine and he wasn't comparing them, but he'd made mistakes before and he didn't want to make one now. The last thing he wanted to do was hurt Beth or himself but the fact of the matter was, he was scared. Scared to take that next step. He'd come this far with Geraldine. He'd confessed his love and had started planning their future together—twice—and it had all ended in misery. Could he do it? Could he take that chance with Beth and start planning their future life together?

The phone on his desk rang and he snatched it up, glad of the interruption. 'Dr Cooper.'

'Ryan.'

'Marty?' Ryan frowned. 'You're on your honeymoon. What's wrong?'

'Nothing's wrong.'

'Then why are you calling me?'

'To see if the house is still standing and that the car is all right. Nat says I'm being paranoid.'

Ryan leaned back in his chair and smiled. 'She's right, cuz. Everything's fine.'

Marty paused. 'And you…and Beth?'

'Good. Fine.' He held his breath, wondering if Marty bought the answer. They knew each other so well and it was rare that they fooled each other.

'Nah.' Marty said after a moment. 'Nice try, but your answers were too quick. You should have paused a little.'

'I'm fine. Beth's fine. Her parents came back from overseas early because Daniel wasn't well. He's had spinal surgery and Phil's fixed everything up. Isabelle's staying at your place with us because people are renting their house.' He tried to sound non-chalant about the whole thing and this time it appeared he'd fooled his cousin.

'Wow. Things move fast, don't they?'

Ryan could hear him quickly relaying the information to Natalie. 'Listen, Marty, you didn't call me to check on the house and car. So what's the deal?'

'Nothing. We were just…discussing you and Beth and how perfect we think you are for each other so we thought we'd give you a quick call to find out if our matchmaking attempt is working. So…you've obviously met Beth's parents.'

'Obviously.'

'And?'

'And they're fantastic people.'

'Excellent. So you and Beth are…fine?'

Ryan chuckled. 'You'd be so happy if I said we were together, wouldn't you? Well, OK, then. Beth and I are together. We're passionately in love, we're looking at a house later this afternoon and should be married before spring arrives.' He said the words in a matter-of-fact tone, hoping the truth would throw Marty into disbelieving every word he'd just uttered. 'Happy now?'

'Yeah. I guess so.'

He could tell by Marty's hesitation that he'd succeeded, and he smiled. 'Good. Now, go back to your bride and make her blush!'

'Well, if you say so. Say hi to Beth for us when you see her next.'

'Will do. Bye.' Ryan put the phone back in the cradle and looked at it for a moment as the words he'd just said to his cousin began to sink in. He shook his head. Oil and water, eh? What about Marty and Natalie? They had allowed business and pleasure to mix and he knew in his heart of hearts that they would make it. They'd already navigated many obstacles and that inner strength would see them through everything.

'So why are you and Beth so different?' As he spoke the question out loud, he realised they weren't. He had a clear picture of the two of them doing exactly what he'd just said to Marty. They'd be passionately in love for the rest of their lives; they'd find the most perfect place to live; and they'd get married, living happily ever after.

Beth wasn't like the Geraldines of this world. She was unique, caring and honest, and he loved every little thing about her. So why had he been trying to stall her since he'd professed his love for her?

'You're a fool,' he uttered, searching around on his desk for a piece of scrap paper and scribbling furiously. 'Hang the paperwork, hang the hospital,' he growled, because what he was doing now was the most important thing he'd ever done in his life.

CHAPTER THIRTEEN

Two hours later, everything was organised.

Ryan picked up the phone and called his secretary for the last time that day. 'Can you find Beth Durant, please? She should be in the spinal ward. Ask her to come to my office and to bring her coat.'

'Anything else?'

'That's it. Is everything else organised?'

'Yes, Sir Ryan.'

'Excellent. Once you've found Beth, go home and enjoy the rest of your Sunday.'

'Yes, Sir Ryan.'

He replaced the phone and began pacing around his office, wondering if what he was doing was going to work. He shoved his hands into his pockets and kept a close eye on the door. This had to work. She had to say yes. It was so important. He had to make sure everything was perfect. He took his hands out of his pockets and looked down at them, amazed to find they were shaking.

'The song!' He stalked back to his desk, picked up the pieces of paper and stuffed them into his jacket pocket. He looked at the door again and wondered impatiently how long it took to walk from the spinal ward to his office. Was she dawdling on purpose?

He raked his hand through his hair. 'Get a grip, Coop.' Taking five deep breaths, he felt more calm, more relaxed, until someone knocked at his door. 'Come in,' he called, and then Beth was there. Standing in his doorway, glaring at him.

'You *summoned* me, Sir Ryan?' Her winter coat was draped over her arm and she was dressed in a pair of boots, designer denims and a cream cashmere top. Her hair was clipped back, revealing the neck he loved to nuzzle. Her mouth was in a grim line and her brown eyes were filled with anger. She'd never looked more incredible and his heart pounded double time with love.

'Thanks for coming.' He stood beside his desk and simply stared at her.

She walked into the room, closing the door behind her. 'Are your hands hurt?'

That was the last thing he'd expected her to say and he actually glanced down at his hands to check. 'No.'

'Then what's wrong with you picking up a phone and calling me yourself?'

'Beth, I—'

'Save it, Ryan. I know you're busy, I know you have a hectic schedule to get through, but if there's nothing wrong with your hands, I'd prefer you to actually make the effort to pick up that phone on your desk and call me *yourself*. If you want to talk to me, you do it directly to me, not through one of your secretaries.' She came to stand before him, dropping her coat onto a nearby chair. 'I am not part of your job.'

'Well, you are in a way and—'

'Not today, Ryan.' She met his gaze. 'I won't have you making me feel as though I'm as insignificant as one of your meetings.'

Ryan swallowed, not realising she'd take it that way.

'Where our relationship is concerned, you and I deal directly with each other. No more notes on the bench. No more phone calls via secretaries. If we're going to make whatever this is between us work, then this is one of the ground rules. You are accountable to me and vice versa.'

'Beth.' He placed his hands on her shoulders and continued to gaze down into her eyes, his voice strong, unwavering. 'You are not insignificant to me.'

'Well, that's exactly how I've felt for the past week, Ryan. You make time to call your office, your mother, the hospital to check on my father, but you don't make the time to call me.'

'I know. I know. You're right.'

Beth felt her heart plummet. 'I am?'

'I was…scared.'

'Of me?' She looked at him incredulously.

'Yes.'

'Why?'

'Because the feelings I have for you are so intense.'

'Oh.' Her heart soared. 'I thought it was because…' She smiled and waved her words away.

'What?'

'Nothing. Never mind.'

'Tell me. Please?'

'I just thought…something had happened while you were in Melbourne. That you'd run into Geraldine and, oh, I don't know, I was being silly. I shouldn't have worried.'

'No. You shouldn't have.' Ryan gathered her close. 'For the record, though, Geraldine wasn't in Melbourne. She's still overseas somewhere and I don't really care where. She's in my past. You're my future.'

Beth gasped and smiled up at him. 'Really?'

'Really.' He placed a quick kiss on her lips. 'Put your coat on. We have somewhere else we need to be.' He picked up her coat and held it out, waiting for her to put her arms into it.

'Ryan, what's going on?'

He picked up his jacket and car keys before holding out a hand to her. 'Do you trust me?'

'Ryan.'

He met her gaze again. 'Do you?'

Beth sighed. 'Yes.'

'Good. Then let's go.' He took her hand and started tugging her out of his office.

'But my parents. They're expecting me back.'

'You can call them.'

'Gee, thanks.' She followed him out of the department and

down the stairs, then out into the cold. They headed over to Marty's four-wheel-drive and Beth was glad she'd opted to wear jeans today. Still, Ryan helped her into the car before closing the door and walking to the driver's side. 'Are you going to tell me what's going on?'

'Nope. It's a surprise.' He put the key in the ignition and started the engine.

Beth's heart, far from plummeting to the depths of despair, was starting to sing. 'But what about your paperwork?'

'Forget about it.'

She raised her eyebrows. 'Lunch with your parents?'

'I've arranged to meet them later.' He reached out and took her hand in his. 'No more questions.'

She shook her head and laughed. 'You have a plane to catch later today. Are you sure you have time for this?'

'I said no more questions, but I'm not going to Perth.'

'What? Ryan!' Beth was stunned. 'Why not?'

'Didn't I just say no more questions?'

'That doesn't mean I can't ask them.'

Ryan shrugged. 'True, but I'm not answering them, and not getting answers will only frustrate you.' He grinned and squeezed her hand. 'Then again, I like it when you're frustrated. Your eyes become this deep chocolate-brown colour and I just want to melt in them.' He paused. 'No wait, they go like that when I kiss you. When you're frustrated they—'

'You're nuts.'

'Yep.' He kissed her hand. 'Nuts about you.'

'Where are we—?'

'Shh.'

'But couldn't you—?'

'Shh.' He smiled at her and she felt her insides turn to mush. Well, she had wanted him to do something spontaneous and out of the ordinary, so why shouldn't she just relax, trust him and enjoy the ride?

Ten minutes later, he pulled into a driveway and cut the engine.

'Do I need to be blindfolded?'

Ryan leaned over and kissed her firmly, a teasing glint in his eyes. 'Only if you want to be.' They both climbed from the car and started walking up to the front door of the house. When Ryan pulled out a key, she was surprised.

'Where are we?'

'My parents' house.'

'What? Are they home?'

'No. I told you I've arranged to meet them later.' When she hesitated at the threshold, Ryan shrugged and scooped her into his arms, carrying her into the house and kicking the door shut. 'I've always wanted to do that.'

'What?'

'Carry the woman I love over the threshold, although the next time it will be…' He stopped, realising he'd almost given it away. Instead, he pressed his lips to hers, loving the way she clung to him, loving the way she responded to him…basically, just loving her.

He carried her into one of the rooms and set her gently on her feet, not breaking the kiss while he enjoyed the way her body felt so perfect against his. He slipped his hands beneath her coat and gently pushed it from her shoulders before gathering her as close as he possibly could. When he reluctantly ended the kiss, she rested her head on his chest, both of them breathing hard. After a minute he pulled back, looking down into her upturned face. 'Come and sit down. I have something I want to play for you.'

Beth glanced around the room and saw a grand piano taking centre stage. 'Wow.'

Ryan removed his jacket and took a few pieces of paper from the inside pocket. 'Bear with me. I haven't written music in a very long time.'

'You wrote music?'

He smiled and pressed a quick kiss to her lips. 'For you.'

'You wrote me a song?' she asked incredulously.

His answer was to sit at the piano and lift the cover off the keys. She sat in the chair closest to the piano and watched as he placed the music on the stand. In the next instant, his clever fingers produced a wonderful, slow, jazzy sound from the amazing instrument and when his smooth voice combined with it, Beth felt tears begin to prick behind her eyes.

You don't seem to mind about my past
The things I've done don't mean a thing
With you I've found a love to last
Through challenges I know we'll face—you give me everything

The strength you give brings me out of hiding
To take off the mask is such a relief
Your true love is so strong and guiding
You give me everything, without censure or grief

We've both been hurt in love before
But now the future's, oh, so clear
Giving, receiving, children…and more
So much to look forward to, year after year

You make me laugh
You make me cry
You twist my insides
You make me high…
Our love will last
The test of time
Say you'll be mine

You don't seem to mind about my past
The things I've done don't mean a thing
With you I've found a love to last
Beth, my love—you give me everything

The entire time he sang, his gaze was glued to hers. Not once did he look at the music or the words he'd written and she knew that every syllable he uttered came from deep within his heart.

When he'd finished, he sat there, looking at her. Slowly, she tood and crossed to his side, sitting down on the stool next to im, her back to the piano so she could look at him with ease.

'That was… Oh, Ryan.' Fresh tears ran down her cheeks and e tenderly brushed them away with his thumb. She leaned towards him and pressed her lips to his, savouring the taste of him.

'I can't believe the way you make me feel,' she whispered against his mouth. 'For so long I was on a merry-go-round, not eally caring how I felt inside. I was undertaking my search for he perfect man and when I'd given up all hope, there you were. Coming into my life, making a difference. I've never known nyone like you. You make me…*feel*. You make me angry, frustrated, amazed, surprised and so much more. All of my emotions re intense and at times overwhelming.'

He nodded and kissed her again.

'The scariest part is that I feel…naked around you. I had this tupid check-list and you just ploughed right through it. You nade me realise I'd been using the check-list to keep myself apart, to not open up, but now there's nowhere for me to hide. At first it was terrifying but now…now I don't want to hide. You've changed me, Ryan. You've made me realise I'm stronger han I thought and that I can accept this rare and precious gift you've offered me. I offer my love back to you. For ever.'

Ryan's response was to kiss her again, savouring the taste of hose words on her lips. Both of them poured their hearts and souls into the kiss, binding them together in a love that would endure for ever.

When they finally came apart, Ryan gazed lovingly at her, his and cupping her face, his thumb gently caressing her cheek. 'I ove you, Beth.' He paused and swallowed. 'Be my wife?' The words were whispered against her mouth and for a moment she couldn't move.

'What did you say?' she breathed, surprise radiating in her quiet tone.

'Be my wife?' he repeated, then he cleared his throat and gave her that slow and sexy smile she adored. 'Marry me, Beth.'

She smiled through her tears. 'Ryan. No one has ever written

a song for me before and I need to say that it's the most romantic thing you could have done. I loved it so much. I love you so
much but…'

'But?'

'Children, Ryan.'

'I want them. I want them with you.'

Beth paused, hoping he didn't take this the wrong way, but
she needed to know. 'And if they have my parents' condition?'

He shrugged. 'So? I love with my heart, just as you do. I don't
care about physical appearance, Beth. I know our children will
have a lot of their mother's qualities, as well as those of her parents and perhaps even some of mine—the good ones, though. If
that's how our kids turn out, they'll be the most amazing children on the planet.'

Beth laughed with relief. 'Really?'

He looked directly into her eyes. 'Really.' His answer was
firm. 'So, do I get an answer? Are you going to marry me?'

'Just you try and stop me.'

It was his turn to chuckle with relief as he settled his mouth
over hers once again. 'I can't get enough of you.'

Beth laughed. 'I know the feeling.' After a while he stood and
helped her to her feet.

'Are we leaving?'

'Yes. We have a few more things to do.'

'Am I allowed to ask what?'

He smiled. 'Yes. First, I'd like you to come look at a house
with me. See if we like it. Then we need to head to the hospital
to see our parents.'

'OK.' She did a double-take. '*Our* parents?'

'Yes. My parents have gone to meet your parents. I must say
my mother was quite taken with you at Natalie and Marty's wedding. She thought you were beautiful and charming and absolutely perfect for me.'

'Oh. Well…er…I guess that's nice to know.'

Ryan smiled as he locked the front door behind him. 'Speaking of the newly-weds, Marty called me this morning.'

'Is everything OK?'

'Yes. Good. Fine.' He smiled as he said the words, and told her about their conversation.

'They're going to be insufferable,' Beth groaned as they reversed out of his parents' driveway.

'They're going to say that they matched us up.'

'For the rest of our lives.' Beth shook her head. 'Both of them, smug and self-righteous know-it-alls, taking complete credit for the way we feel about each other. I can just hear them now. "We knew from the first moment that you two would be perfect for each other,"' she mimicked, then laughed, unable to believe she could be this happy.

Ryan glanced across at the woman he loved, the woman who had changed him for ever. He took Beth's hand in his and placed a tender kiss on it. 'Yes. We are perfect for each other. In fact, I think we should thank them for their so-called matchmaking.'

Beth kissed his hand in return. 'Why, Sir Ryan, I couldn't agree more.'

0406/03a

MILLS & BOON

Live the emotion

_Medical
romance™

HIS HONOURABLE SURGEON by *Kate Hardy*

The Honourable Victoria Radley is devoted to
her patients – there's no time for love in her life.
Consultant neurologist Jake Lewis is drawn to
Vicky, but when a sudden life-threatening condition
threatens their relationship Vicky realises that Jake is
the only one who can help her...

POSH DOCS Honourable, eligible, and in demand!

PREGNANT WITH HIS CHILD by *Lilian Darcy*

Flight doctors Christina Farrelly and Joe Barrett
have been in love for years. Joe spends a week every
month at the Crocodile Creek Medical Centre,
where Christina works. Christina wants all of Joe
– or nothing. But it is only after she tells him it is
over, she discovers she is pregnant...

CROCODILE CREEK: 24-HOUR RESCUE
A cutting-edge medical centre.
Fully equipped for saving lives and loves!

THE CONSULTANT'S ADOPTED SON
by *Jennifer Taylor*

Nurse Rose Tremayne would have done anything to
keep her baby, but circumstances forced her into
adoption, but she's never stopped wondering what
happened to her precious little boy... Then Rose
finds herself working with Owen Gallagher – her
son's adopted father...

Bachelor Dads – Single Doctors...Single Fathers!

On sale 5th May 2006

Available at WHSmith, Tesco, ASDA, Borders, Eason,
Sainsbury's and most bookshops

www.millsandboon.co.uk

MILLS & BOON®

Live the emotion

Medical romance™

HER LONGED-FOR FAMILY by Josie Metcalfe

Doctor Nick Howell has never forgiven Libby for running out on him – until she turns up as the new A&E doctor and it becomes clear that an accident and resulting amnesia has cut out part of her life. Now it's up to Nick to help her remember...

The ffrench Doctors – a family of doctors – all in the family way

MISSION: MOUNTAIN RESCUE
by Amy Andrews

Army medic Richard Hollingsworth has devoted his life to saving others. But his medical skills have put his life in danger – and that of his beloved Holly. Now, to escape their mountain captors, they must submit to the bond they once shared...

24:7 Feel the heat – every hour...every minute... every heartbeat

THE GOOD FATHER by Maggie Kingsley

Neonatologist Gabriel Dalgleish is passionate about his tiny patients. It seems as if they are all he cares for. Except for Maddie. The new medical secretary slips through Gabriel's defences, right to his vulnerable heart!

THE BABY DOCTORS
Making families is their business!

On sale 5th May 2006

Available at WHSmith, Tesco, ASDA, Borders, Eason, Sainsbury's and most bookshops

www.millsandboon.co.uk

0406/03b

006/05a

MILLS & BOON®

Live the emotion

In May 2006, By Request presents two
collections of three favourite romances by
our bestselling Mills & Boon authors:

Australian Playboy Tycoons

by Miranda Lee

The Playboy's Proposition
The Playboy's Virgin
The Playboy in Pursuit

Make sure you buy these irresistible stories!

On sale 5th May 2006

*Available at WHSmith, Tesco, ASDA, Borders, Eason,
Sainsbury's and most bookshops*

www.millsandboon.co.uk

MILLS & BOON®

Live the emotion

006/05b

Convenient Weddings

A Husband of Convenience
by Jacqueline Baird
A Passionate Surrender by Helen Bianchin
Bride for a Year by Kathryn Ross

**Make sure you buy these
irresistible stories!**

On sale 5th May 2006

*Available at WHSmith, Tesco, ASDA, Borders, Eason,
Sainsbury's and most bookshops*

www.millsandboon.co.uk

Part basset, part beagle, all Cupid... can a matchmaking hound fetch a new love for his owner?

For Nina Askew, turning forty means freedom – from the ex-husband, from their stuffy suburban home. Freedom to have her own apartment in the city, freedom to focus on what *she* wants for a change. And what she wants is a bouncy puppy to cheer her up. Instead she gets...Fred.

Overweight, smelly and obviously suffering from some kind of doggy depression, Fred is light-years from perky. But for all his faults, he does manage to put Nina face-to-face with Alex Moore, her gorgeous younger neighbour...

On sale 5th May 2006
Don't miss out!

Available at WHSmith, Tesco, ASDA, Borders, Eason, Sainsbury's and all good paperback bookshops

www.millsandboon.co.uk

0506/055/MB033

There's a mystery around every corner...

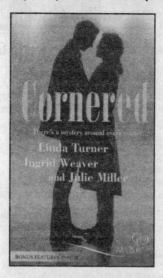

FOOLING AROUND by Linda Turner
Before inheriting a detective agency, Josie London's only adventures came courtesy of her favourite books. Now she was donning disguises and teaming up with Willey Valentine to trail a mobster.

THE MAN IN THE SHADOWS by Ingrid Weaver
Detective Sloan Morrissey has been missing for a year, but private investigator Erika Balogh is sure she's spotted him on the streets and inhaled his scent in her bedroom. Is her lover still alive?

A MIDSUMMER NIGHT'S MURDER by Julie Miller
When English professor Hannah Greene sets off on a wilderness hike, she doesn't expect people to start dying. To stay alive, she'll have to work with guide Rafe Kincaid and find the killer among them.

On sale 21st April 2006

Available at WHSmith, Tesco, ASDA, Borders, Eason, Sainsbury's and all good paperback bookshops

www.millsandboon.co.uk

4 FREE

BOOKS AND A SURPRISE GIFT!

We would like to take this opportunity to thank you for reading this Mills & Boon® book by offering you the chance to take FOUR more specially selected titles from the Medical Romance™ series absolutely FREE! We're also making this offer to introduce you to the benefits of the Reader Service™—

- ★ FREE home delivery
- ★ FREE gifts and competitions
- ★ FREE monthly Newsletter
- ★ Exclusive Reader Service offers
- ★ Books available before they're in the shops

Accepting these FREE books and gift places you under no obligation to buy. you may cancel at any time. even after receiving your free shipment. Simply complete your details below and return the entire page to the address below. You don't even need a stamp!

YES! Please send me 4 free Medical Romance books and a surprise gift. I understand that unless you hear from me. I will receive 6 superb new titles every month for just £2.80 each, postage and packing free. I am under no obligation to purchase any books and may cancel my subscription at any time. The free books and gift will be mine to keep in any case.

M6ZED

Ms/Mrs/Miss/Mr ....Initials ....
BLOCK CAPITALS PLEASE

Surname ....

Address ....

....

....Postcode................................

Send this whole page to:
UK: FREEPOST CN8I, Croydon, CR9 3WZ

Offer valid in UK only and is not available to current Reader service subscribers to this series. Overseas and Eire please write for details. We reserve the right to refuse an application and applicants must be aged 18 years or over. Only one application per household. Terms and prices subject to change without notice. Offer expires 3Ist July 2006. As a result of this application. you may receive offers from Harlequin Mills & Boon and other carefully selected companies. If you would prefer not to share in this opportunity please write to The Data Manager. PO Box 676, Richmond, TW9 IWU.

Mills & Boon® is a registered trademark owned by Harlequin Mills & Boon Limited.
Medical Romance™ is being used as a trademark. The Reader Service™ is being used as a trademark.